16/12/4

CHURCH END

KU-071-656

020

Please return/renew this item by the
last date shown to avoid a charge.
Books may also be renewed by phone
and Internet. May not be renewed if
required by another reader.

www.libraries.barnet.gov.uk

LONDON BOROUGH

30131 05651145 1

LONDON BOROUGH OF BARNET

www.randomhousechildrens.co.uk

THE
EIGHTEENTH
EMERGENCY

Betsy Byars

RED FOX

THE EIGHTEENTH EMERGENCY
A RED FOX BOOK 978 1 782 95534 4

Published in Great Britain by Red Fox,
an imprint of Random House Children's Publishers UK
A Penguin Random House Company

Penguin
Random House
UK

First published in Great Britain by The Bodley Head, 1974

This edition published 2015

5 7 9 10 8 6 4

Copyright © Betsy Byars, 1973
Illustrations copyright © Quentin Blake, 1974

The right of Betsy Byars to be identified as the author of this work has been asserted
in accordance with the Copyright, Designs and Patents Act 1988.

All rights reserved. No part of this publication may be reproduced, stored in a retrieval system,
or transmitted in any form or by any means, electronic, mechanical, photocopying,
recording or otherwise, without the prior permission of the publishers.

Penguin Random House is committed to a sustainable future for
our business, our readers and our planet. This book is made from
Forest Stewardship Council® certified paper.

MIX
Paper from
responsible sources
FSC® C018179

Typeset in Minister light 11/18pt by Falcon Oast Graphic Art Ltd

Red Fox Books are published by Random House Children's Publishers UK,
61–63 Uxbridge Road, London W5 5SA

www.randomhousechildrens.co.uk
www.totallyrandombooks.co.uk
www.randomhouse.co.uk

Addresses for companies within The Random House Group Limited can be found at:
www.randomhouse.co.uk/offices.htm

THE RANDOM HOUSE GROUP Limited Reg. No. 954009

A CIP catalogue record for this book is available from the British Library.

Printed and bound in Great Britain by Clays Ltd, St Ives plc

Contents

Chapter One

THE pigeons flew out of the alley in one long swoop and settled on the awning of the grocery store. A dog ran out of the alley with a torn Cracker Jack box in his mouth. Then came the boy.

The boy was running hard and fast. He stopped at the sidewalk, looked both ways, saw that the street was deserted and kept going. The dog caught the boy's fear, and he started running with him.

The two of them ran together for a block. The dog's legs were so short he appeared to be on wheels. His Cracker Jack box was hitting the sidewalk. He kept glancing at the boy because he didn't know why they were running. The boy knew. He did not even notice the dog beside him or the trail of spilled Cracker Jacks behind.

Suddenly the boy slowed down, went up some stairs and entered an apartment building. The dog stopped. He sensed that the danger had passed, but he stood for a moment at the bottom of the stairs. Then he went back to eat the Cracker Jacks scattered on the sidewalk and to snarl at the pigeons who had flown down to get some.

Inside the building the boy was still running. He went up the stairs three at a time, stumbled, pulled himself up by the banister and kept going until he was safely inside his own apartment. Then he sagged against the door.

His mother was sitting on the sofa, going over some papers. The boy waited for her to look up and ask him what had happened. He thought she should be able to hear something was wrong just from the terrible way he was breathing. 'Mom,' he said.

'Just a minute. I've got to get these orders straight.' When she went over her cosmetic orders she had a dedicated, scientific look. He waited until she came to the end of the sheet.

'Mom.' Without looking up, she turned to the next page. He said again, '*Mom.*'

'I'm almost through. There's a mistake some—'

He said, 'Never mind.' He walked heavily through the living room and into the hall. He threw himself down on the day bed.

His mother said, 'I'm almost through with this, Benjie.'

'I said, "Never mind."' He looked up at the ceiling. In a blur he saw a long cobweb hanging by the light fixture. A month ago he had climbed on a chair, written UNSAFE FOR PUBLIC SWINGING and drawn an arrow to the cobweb. It was still there.

He closed his eyes. He was breathing so hard his throat hurt.

'Benjie, come back,' his mother called. 'I'm through.'

'Never mind.'

'Come on, Benjie, I want to talk to you.'

He got up slowly and walked into the living room. She had put her order books on the coffee table. 'Sit down. Tell me what's wrong.' He hesitated and then sat beside her on the sofa. She waited and then said again, 'What's wrong?'

He did not answer for a moment. He looked out of the window, and he could see the apartment across the street. A yellow cat was sitting in the window watching the pigeons. He said in a low voice, 'Some boys are going to kill me.'

'Not *kill* you, Benjie,' she said. 'No one is—'

He glanced quickly at her. 'Well, how do I know what they're going to do?' he said, suddenly angry. 'They're chasing me, that's all I know. When you see somebody chasing you, and when it's Marv Hammerman and Tony Lionni and a boy in a black sweatshirt you don't stop and say, "Now, what *exactly* are you guys planning to do – kill me or just break a few arms and legs?"'

'What did you do to these boys?'

'What did *I* do? I didn't do anything. You think I would do something to Marv Hammerman who is the biggest boy in my school? He is

5

bigger than the eighth graders. He should be in high school.'

'I know you did something. I can always tell. Now, what happened?'

'Nothing, Mom. I didn't do anything.' He looked down at his shoes. With his foot he began to kick at the rug. A little mound of red lint piled up in front of his tennis shoe.

'They wouldn't be after you for nothing.'

'Well, they are.' He paused. He knew he had to give an explanation, but he could not give the right one. He said, 'Maybe Hammerman just doesn't like me. I don't know. I'm not a mind reader.'

'Look at me, Benjie.'

Without looking up he said, 'Mom, just listen to what Hammerman did to this boy in my room one time. This boy was in line in the cafeteria and Hammerman came up to him and—'

'What I want to hear is what happened *today*, Benjie.'

'Just *listen*. And this boy in the cafeteria was standing in line, Mom, doing absolutely nothing, and Hammerman comes up to him and—'

'Benjie, what happened *today*?'

He hesitated. He looked down at his tennis shoe. There was a frayed hole in the toe, and he had taken a ballpoint pen and written AIR VENT and drawn a little arrow pointing to the hole.

'What happened?' she asked again.

'Nothing.' He did not look at her.

'Benjie—'

'Nothing happened.'

She sighed, then abruptly she looked up. 'The beans!' She walked to the kitchen, and he lay back on the sofa and closed his eyes.

'Benjie?' He looked up. His mother was leaning around the door, looking at him. 'Why

7

don't you watch television? Get your mind off yourself. That always helps me.'

'No, it won't help.'

'Well, let's just see what's on.' She came back in, turned on the television and waited for the set to warm up. He closed his eyes. He knew there was nothing on television that could interest him.

'Tarzan!' his mother said. 'You always have loved Tarzan.'

He opened his eyes and glanced at the screen. In the depths of the jungle, a hunter had stumbled into quicksand, and Tarzan was swinging to the rescue.

'All the hunter has to do,' he said with a disgusted sigh, 'is lie down on the quicksand and not struggle and he won't sink.'

'That wouldn't leave anything for Tarzan to do though, would it?' his mother said, smiling a little.

'Oh, I don't know.' He closed his eyes and shifted on the sofa. After a minute he heard his mother go back into the kitchen. He opened his eyes. On the screen the hunter was still struggling. Cheetah was beginning to turn nervous somersaults. Tarzan was getting closer.

Once he and his friend Ezzie had made a list of all the ways they knew to stay alive. Ezzie had claimed he could stay alive in the jungle for ever. Ezzie said every jungle emergency had a simple solution.

Lying on the sofa, he tried to remember some of those old emergencies.

A second one came into his mind. Emergency Two – Attack by an Unfriendly Lion. Lion attack, Ezzie claimed, was an everyday occurrence in the jungle. What you had to do to survive was wait until the last moment, until the lion was upon you, and then you had to ram your arm all the way down the lion's throat. This would choke him and make him helpless. It was bound to be a little unpleasant, Ezzie admitted, to be up to your shoulder in lion, but that couldn't be helped.

'Is the Tarzan movie any good?' his mother asked from the kitchen.

'No.' He reached out with his foot and turned off the television. He sighed. Nothing could take his mind off Marv Hammerman for long.

'If it makes you feel any better,' his mother said, 'Teddy Roosevelt had the same problem. I saw it on television. Boys used to pick on him and chase him.'

'No, it doesn't,' he said. He waited a minute and then asked, 'What did Teddy Roosevelt do about it?'

'Well, as I remember it, Teddy's father got him a gymnasium and Teddy exercised and got strong and nobody ever picked on him again.'

'Oh.'

'Of course, it wasn't the same as—'

'Don't bother getting me a gymnasium.'

'Now, Benjie, I didn't—'

'Unless you know of some exerciser that gives instant muscles.' He thought about it for a minute. He would go out, exerciser in his pocket, and say, 'Here I am, Hammerman.' Then, just when Hammerman was stepping towards him, he would whip out the exerciser, pump it once, and muscles would pop out all over his body like balloons.

'Well, you'll handle it,' his mother said. 'In a few weeks you'll look back on this and laugh.'

'Sure.'

He lay with his eyes closed, trying to remember some more of the old ways he and Ezzie knew to survive life's greatest emergencies.

Emergency Three – Unexpected Charge of

an Enraged Bull. Bulls have a blind spot in the centre of their vision, so when being charged by a bull, you try to line yourself up with this blind spot.

'Fat people can't do it, Mouse,' Ezzie had told him. 'That's why you never see any fat bullfighters. You and I can. We just turn sideways like this, see, get in the blind spot and wait.'

He could remember exactly how Ezzie had looked, waiting sideways in the blind spot of the imaginary bull. 'And there's one other thing,' Ezzie had added. 'It will probably work for a rhinoceros too.'

Emergency Four – Crocodile Attack. When attacked by a crocodile, prop a stick in its mouth and the crocodile is helpless.

At one time this had been his own favourite emergency. He had spent a lot of time dreaming of tricking crocodiles. He had imagined himself a tornado in the water, handing out the sticks like party favours. 'Take that and that and that!' The stunned crocodiles, mouths propped open, had dragged themselves away. For the rest of their lives they had avoided children with sticks in their hands. 'Hey, no!' his dream crocodiles had cried, 'let that kid alone. He's got sticks, man, *sticks!*'

Abruptly he turned his head towards the sofa. The smile which had come to his face when he had remembered the crocodiles now faded. He pulled a thread in the slip cover. The material began to pucker, and he stopped pulling and smoothed it out. Then he took a pencil from his pocket and wrote in tiny letters on the wall PULL THREAD IN CASE OF BOREDOM and drew a little arrow to the sofa.

The words blurred suddenly, and he let the pencil drop behind the sofa. He lay back down.

Hammerman was in his mind again, and he closed his eyes. He tried hard to think of the days when he and Ezzie had been ready to handle crocodiles and bulls, quicksand and lions. It seemed a long time ago.

Chapter Two

'*HEY* Mouse!' It was Ezzie.

He got up from the sofa quickly and went to the window. 'What?' he called back.

'Come on down.'

His mother said in the kitchen, 'You've got to eat.'

'I've got to eat, Ezzie.'

'Well, hurry up. I'll wait.'

He stood at the window and watched Ezzie

sit down on the steps. The dog had finished with his Cracker Jacks and was now sitting in front of Ezzie, looking at him hopefully. The smell of chicken and noodles was coming from one of the windows, and the dog thought it was coming from Ezzie. The dog wanted some chicken and noodles so badly that his nose had started to run.

Ezzie patted the dog once. 'I haven't got anything,' he told him. 'And quit looking at me.' Once the dog had looked at Ezzie so long that Ezzie had gone in the house and fixed him a deviled egg sandwich. 'I haven't got anything,' Ezzie said again and turned his head away. Ezzie had named the dog Garbage Dog because of his eating habits. 'Go *on*.' Slowly Garbage Dog got up. He circled once like a radar finder and then began slowly to move in the direction of the chicken and noodles.

'Come to supper,' Mouse's mother called.

He went into the kitchen where his mother was putting the food on the table. She sat down, spread a paper napkin on her lap and said, 'Why doesn't Ezzie help you with those boys?'

'What?'

'Why doesn't Ezzie help you fight those boys?' she repeated, nodding her head towards the window.

'Oh, Mom.'

'I mean it. If there were *two* of you, then those boys would think twice before—'

'Oh, Mom!' He bent over his plate and began to smash his lima beans with his fork. He thought about it for a moment, of stepping in front of Marv Hammerman and Tony Lionni and the boy in the black sweatshirt and saying in a cool voice, 'I think I'd better warn you that I've got my friend with me.'

'Who's your friend?'

'*This* is my friend.' At that Ezzie would step out from the shadows and stand with him.

Marv Hammerman would look at them, sizing them up, the two of them, this duo his mother had created for strength. Then with a faint smile Hammerman would reach out, grab them up like cymbals and clang them together. When Hammerman set them down they would twang for forty-five minutes before they could stumble off.

'Well, I know what I'm talking about, that's all,' his mother said. 'If you could get Ezzie to help you—'

'All right, Mom, I'll ask him.'

He ate four lima beans and looked at his mother. 'Is that enough? I'm not hungry.'

'Eat.'

He thought he was going to choke. Emergency Five – Being Choked by a Boa Constrictor. When you were being strangled by a boa constrictor, Ezzie had said, what you had to do was taunt the boa constrictor and get him to *bite* you instead of *strangle* you. His bite, Ezzie admitted, was a little painful but the strangulation was worse.

This had seemed a first-rate survival measure at the time. Now he had trouble imagining him and Ezzie in the jungle being squeezed by the boa constrictor. He tried to imagine Ezzie's face, pink and earnest, above the boa constrictor's loop. He tried to hear Ezzie's voice taunting, 'Sure you can strangle, but can you bite? Let's see you try to bite us!'

'Hey, Mouse, you coming?' Ezzie had opened the door to the hall now, and his voice came up the stairs as if through a megaphone.

'I'll eat the rest later,' Mouse said. He was already out of his chair, moving towards the door.

'Oh, all right,' his mother said, 'go on.'

He ran quickly out of the apartment and down the stairs. Ezzie was waiting for him outside, sitting down. As soon as he saw Mouse, Ezzie got up and said, 'Hey, what happened? Where'd you go after school?'

Mouse said, 'Hammerman's after me.'

Ezzie's pink mouth formed a perfect O. He didn't say anything, but his breath came out in a long sympathetic wheeze. Finally he said, '*Marv* Hammerman?' even though he knew there was only one Hammerman in the world, just as there had been only one Hitler.

'Yes.'

'Is after *you?*'

Mouse nodded, sunk in misery. He could see Marv Hammerman. He came up in Mouse's mind the way monsters do in horror movies, big and powerful, with the same cold, unreal eyes. It was the eyes Mouse really feared. One look from those eyes, he thought, just one look of a certain length – about three seconds – and you knew you were his next victim.

'What did you do?' Ezzie asked. 'Or did you do anything?'

At least, Mouse thought, Ezzie understood that. If you were Marv Hammerman, you didn't need a reason. He sat down on the steps and squinted up at Ezzie. 'I did something,' he said.

'What?' Ezzie asked. His tongue flicked out and in so quickly it didn't even moisten his lips. 'What'd you do? You bump into him or something?'

Mouse shook his head.

'Well, what?'

Mouse said, 'You know that big chart in the upstairs hall at school?'

'What'd you say? I can't even hear you, Mouse. You're muttering.' Ezzie bent closer. 'Look at me. Now what did you say?'

Mouse looked up, still squinting. He said, 'You know that big chart outside the history room? In the hall?'

'Chart?' Ezzie said blankly. 'What chart, Mouse?'

'This chart takes up the whole wall, Ez, how could you miss it? It's a chart about early man, and it shows man's progress up from the apes, the side view of all those different kinds of prehistoric men, like Cro-Magnon man and Homo erectus. *That* chart.'

'Oh, yeah, I saw it, so go on.'

Mouse could see that Ezzie was eager for him to get on to the good part, the violence. He slumped. He wet his lips. He said, 'Well, when I was passing this chart on my way out of history – and I don't know why I did this – I really don't. When I was passing this chart, Ez, on my way to math—' He swallowed, almost choking on his spit. 'When I was passing this chart, Ez, I took my pencil and I wrote Marv Hammerman's name on the bottom of the chart and then I drew an arrow to the picture of Neanderthal man.'

'What?' Ezzie cried. *'What?'* He could not seem to take it in. Mouse knew that Ezzie had been prepared to sympathize with an accident. He had almost been the victim of one of those himself. One day at school Ezzie had reached for the handle on the water fountain a second ahead of Marv Hammerman. If Ezzie hadn't glanced up just in time, seen Hammerman and said quickly, 'Go ahead, I'm not thirsty,' then this sagging figure on the steps might be him. 'What did you do it for, Mouse?'

'I don't know.'

'You crazy or something?'

'I don't know.'

'Marv Hammerman!' Ezzie sighed. It was a

mournful sound that seemed to have come from a culture used to sorrow. 'Anybody else in the school would have been better. I would rather have the principal after me than Marv Hammerman.'

'I know.'

'Hammerman's big, Mouse. He's flunked a lot.'

'I know,' Mouse said again. There was an unwritten law that it was all right to fight anyone in your own grade. The fact that Hammerman was older and stronger made no difference. They were both in the sixth grade.

'Then what'd you do it for?' Ezzie asked.

'I don't know.'

'You must want trouble,' Ezzie said. 'Like my grandfather. He's always provoking people. The bus driver won't even pick him up any more.'

'No, I don't want trouble.'

'Then, why did you—'

'I don't *know*.' Then he sagged again and said, 'I didn't even know I had done it, really, until I'd finished. I just looked at the picture of Neanderthal man and thought of Hammerman. It does look like him, Ezzie, the sloping face and the shoulders.'

'Maybe Hammerman doesn't know you did it though,' Ezzie said. 'Did you ever think of that? I mean, who's going to go up to Hammerman and tell him his name is on the prehistoric man chart?' Ezzie leaned forward. 'Hey, Hammerman,' he said, imitating the imaginary fool, 'I saw a funny thing about you on the prehistoric man chart! Now, who in their right mind is going to—'

'He was right behind me when I did it,' Mouse said.

'What?'

'He was right behind me,' Mouse said stiffly. He could remember turning and looking into Hammerman's eyes. It was such a strange, troubling moment that Mouse was unable to think about it.

Ezzie's mouth formed the O, made the sympathetic sigh. Then he said, 'And you don't even know what you did it for?'

'No.'

Ezzie sank down on the steps beside Mouse. He leaned over his knees and said, 'You ought to get out of that habit, that writing names and drawing arrows, you know that? I see those arrows everywhere. I'll be walking down the street and I'll look on a building and I'll see the word DOOR written in little letters and there'll be an arrow pointing to the door and I know you did it. It's crazy, labelling stuff like that.'

'I never did that, Ez, not to a door.'

'Better to a door, if you ask me,' Ezzie said, shaking his head. He paused for a moment, then asked in a lower voice, 'You ever been hit before, Mouse? I mean, hard?'

Mouse sighed. The conversation had now passed beyond the question of whether Hammerman would attack. It was now a matter of whether he, Mouse Fawley, could survive the attack. He said thickly, remembering, 'Four times.'

'Four times in one fight? I mean, you stood up for four hits, Mouse?' There was grudging admiration in his voice.

Mouse shook his head. 'Four hits – four fights.'

'You went right down each time? I mean, POW and you went down, POW and you went down, POW and you went—'

'Yes!'

'Where did you take these hits?' Ezzie asked, straightening suddenly. Ezzie had never taken a single direct blow in his life because he was a

27

good dodger. Sometimes his mother chased him through the apartment striking at him while he dodged and ducked, crying, 'Look out, Mom, look out now! You're going to hit me!'

He asked again, 'Where were you hit?'

Mouse said, 'In the stomach.'

'All four times?'

'Yeah.' Mouse suddenly thought of his stomach as having a big red circular target on it with HIT HERE printed in the centre.

'Who hit you?'

'Two boys in Cincinnati when I was on vacation, and a boy named Mickey Swearinger, and somebody else I don't remember.' He lowered his head because he remembered the fourth person all right, but he didn't want to tell Ezzie about it. If he had added the name of Viola Angotti to the list of those who had hit him in the stomach, Ezzie's face would have screwed up with laughter.

'Viola Angotti hit you? No fooling, Viola Angotti?' It was the sort of thing Ezzie could carry on about for hours. 'Viola Angotti. *The* Viola Angotti?'

And Mouse would have had to keep sitting there saying over and over, 'Yes, Viola Angotti hit me in the stomach. Yes, *the* Viola Angotti.' And then he would have to tell Ezzie all about it, every detail, how one recess long ago the boys had decided to put some girls in the school trash cans. It had been one of those suggestions that stuns everyone with its rightness. Someone had said, 'Hey, let's put those girls over there in the trash cans!' and the plan won immediate acceptance. Nothing could have been more appropriate. The trash cans were big and had just been emptied, and in an instant the boys were off chasing the girls and yelling at the top of their lungs.

It had been wonderful at first, Mouse remembered. Primitive blood had raced through his body. The desire to capture had driven him like a wild man through the school yard, up the sidewalk, everywhere. He understood what had driven the caveman and the barbarian, because this same passion was driving him. Putting the girls in the trash cans was the most important challenge of his life. His long screaming charge ended with him red-faced, gasping for breath – and with Viola Angotti pinned against the garbage cans.

His moment of triumph was short. It lasted about two seconds. Then it began to dim as he realized, first, that it *was* Viola Angotti, and, second, that he was not going to be able to get her into the garbage can without a great deal of help.

He cried, 'Hey, you guys, come on, I've got one,' but behind him the school yard was silent. Where was everybody? he had wondered uneasily. As it turned out, the principal had caught the other boys, and they were all being marched back in the front door of the school, but Mouse didn't know this.

He called again, 'Come on, you guys, get the lid off this garbage can, will you?'

And then, when he said that, Viola Angotti had taken two steps forward. She said, 'Nobody's putting *me* in no garbage can.' He could still remember how she had looked standing there. She had recently taken the part of the Statue of Liberty in a class play, and somehow she seemed taller and stronger at this moment than when she had been in costume.

He cried, 'Hey, you guys!' It was a plea. 'Where are you?'

And then Viola Angotti had taken one more step, and with a faint sigh she had socked him in the stomach so hard that he had doubled over and lost his lunch. He hadn't known it was possible to be hit like that outside a boxing ring. It was the hardest blow he had ever taken. Viola Angotti could be heavyweight champion of the world.

As she walked past his crumpled body she had said again, 'Nobody's putting me in no garbage can.' It had sounded like one of the world's basic truths. The sun will rise. The tides will flow. Nobody's putting Viola Angotti in no garbage can.

Later, when he thought about it, he realized that he had been lucky. If she had wanted to, Viola Angotti could have capped her victory by tossing his rag-doll body into the garbage can and slamming down the lid. Then, when the principal came out onto the playground calling, 'Benjamin Fawley! Has anybody seen Benjamin Fawley?' he would have had to moan, 'I'm in here.' He would have had to climb out of the garbage can in front of the whole school. His shame would have followed him for life. When he was a grown man, people would still be pointing him out to their children.

'*That's* the man that Viola Angotti stuffed into the garbage can.'

Now he thought that Marv Hammerman could make Viola Angotti's blow seem like a baby's pat. He wanted to double over on the steps.

Ezzie said, 'You ought to watch out for your stomach like a fighter, protect your body. There's a lot of valuable stuff in there.'

'I know.'

'The trick of it,' Ezzie said, 'is moving quickly, ducking, getting out of the way.' Ezzie did a few quick steps, his feet flashing on the sidewalk. 'You dance, Mouse, like this.' Mouse suddenly remembered that Ezzie had once told him that if you were ever bitten by a tarantula (Emergency Six) you had to start dancing immediately. Ezzie said you were supposed to do this special Italian folk dance, but any quick lively steps would probably do.

Mouse had a picture of himself doing this lively dance in front of Hammerman. Hammerman would watch for a moment. There would be no expression on his face. The dance would reach a peak. Mouse's arms and legs would be a blur of motion. And then Hammerman would reach down, a sort of slow graceful movement like he was bowling, and come up effortlessly right into Mouse's stomach.

Mouse leaned forward, shielding his body with his arms. He cleared his throat. 'Did anybody ever hit you, Ezzie?'

Ezzie stopped dancing. 'Sure.'

'Who?'

'Well, relatives mostly. You can't hardly walk through my living room without somebody trying to hit you – for any little thing. I accidentally step on my sister's feet – she's got long feet, Mouse, she can't hardly buy ordinary shoes, and she takes

34

it as an insult if you step on one of them. She's fast too, Mouse. That's how I learned about getting out of the way.'

'But nobody like Hammerman ever hit you?'

'No.' He sounded apologetic.

Mouse sighed. Above him his mother called, 'Benjie, come up now. I want you to do something for me.'

'I got to go.' Mouse still sat there. He hated to leave the warmth of Ezzie's understanding. Ezzie didn't want to leave either. Mouse had taken on a fine tragic dimension in his eyes, and there was something about being with a person like that that made him feel good.

Ezzie had felt the same way about their teacher last fall when he had told them he had to go to the hospital. For the first time, Mr. Stein in his baggy suit had seemed a fine tragic figure, bigger than life. Ezzie would have done anything for Mr. Stein that day. But then, when Mr. Stein came limping back the next week – it turned out he had had some bone spurs removed from his heels – he had been his normal size.

'Benjie, come up now,' his mother called again.

'I'm coming.'

'Did you tell your mom about Hammerman being after you?' Ezzie asked.

'Yeah.'

'What'd she say?'

He tried to think of the most impossible statement his mother had made. 'She said I'll laugh about it in a week or two.'

'Laugh about it?'

'Yeah, through my bandages.'

Ezzie's face twisted into a little smile. 'Hey, remember Al Armsby when he had those broken ribs? Remember how he would beg us not to make him laugh? And I had this one joke about a monkey and I would keep telling it and keep telling it and he was practically on his knees begging for mercy and—'

Mouse got slowly to his feet. 'Well, I better go,' he said.

Ezzie stopped smiling. 'Hey, wait a minute. Listen, I just remembered something. I know a boy that Hammerman beat up, and he said it wasn't so bad.'

'Who?'

'A friend of my brother's. I'll find out about it and let you know.'

'All right,' Mouse said. He did not allow himself to believe it was true. Sometimes Ezzie lied like this out of sympathy. If you said, 'My stomach hurts and I think I'm going to die,' and if Ezzie really liked you, he would say, 'I know a boy whose stomach hurt worse than that and *he*

37

didn't die!' And if you said, 'Who?' Ezzie would say, 'A friend of my brother's.' Ezzie brother only had one friend that Mouse knew about, and this friend would have had to have daily brushes with death to fulfil all of Ezzie's statements.

Still, it made Mouse want to cry for a moment that Ezzie would lie to spare him. Or maybe he wanted to cry because Hammerman was going to kill him. He didn't know. He said, 'Thanks, Ez,' in a choked voice. He turned and walked quickly into the apartment building.

Chapter Three

MOUSE was just starting up the stairs when his mother and Mrs. Casino from across the hall came out of the apartment. 'Wait a minute, Benjie,' his mother said. 'Mrs. Casino wants to know if you'll walk up to Margy's and get Mr. Casino. She'd do it but she's keeping the baby for Agnes tonight.'

Mrs. Casino's round face was worried.

She was holding her apron up in both hands. She said, 'You mind, Benjie?'

He minded and he wanted them to know it. He sighed and looked down at his feet, at the vent hole in the toe of his shoe. Then he glanced up at the wall. There was a long crack in the plaster, and two months ago Mouse had written TO OPEN BUILDING TEAR ALONG THIS LINE and drawn an arrow to the crack. He turned his head away. He thought suddenly that Ezzie was right. He shouldn't draw those arrows everywhere.

'Well?' his mother said.

'Oh, all right.' Mouse turned and started down the stairs, his shoulders hanging. He knew this gave him a dejected look because his mother was always telling him in such a stern way to hold up his shoulders.

'You're a good boy, Benjie,' Mrs. Casino

called, then she said loudly to his mother, 'You got a good boy there. That's one boy we don't have to worry about in this world.'

His mother called, 'Just go right straight there and back, Benjie.'

'All right.'

'And don't rush Mr. Casino.'

'He won't rush him,' Mrs. Casino said confidently.

Mouse went out the door, slamming it behind him, and started up the street. The sun had disappeared in the few minutes he had been inside, and now the street was darker, colder. Pigeons were going to roost over the grocery store, their wings pale against the dark brick. Mouse zipped up his jacket.

A block ahead he could see Ezzie running. Ezzie and his five sisters and brother had to be there when Ezzie's father got home from work.

It didn't matter what they did during the day as long as all seven of them were there waiting at the day's end.

Mouse called, 'Hey, Ez! Ezzie!' Ezzie turned and Mouse said, 'Wait up.'

Ezzie pointed to his arm where a watch would have been if he had had one. Mouse nodded and waved him on and then walked slowly up the street.

He started thinking again about Marv Hammerman. In his mind he could see Hammerman exactly as he had looked after school that afternoon. Mouse hadn't gotten around to telling Ezzie about that.

Mouse had come out of school so fast he had almost pushed two girls down the steps. He wanted only to get home before Hammerman saw him.

'Watch it, Benjie,' the biggest girl, Rebecca,

had said, straightening angrily.

He had muttered, 'Sorry,' and had run ahead of them a few steps. Then he came to a halt. At the bottom of the steps was Marv Hammerman, waiting.

There was something animal-like about Hammerman with his long limbs and careless grace, his clothes that fitted as if they were an extra skin, the shaggy hair that appeared never to have known the pull of a comb. Hammerman had been watching for Mouse, and his eyes got a little brighter when he saw him.

'I thought you were in such a big hurry,' Rebecca said scornfully, nudging him in the back with her books as she passed. Mouse hardly noticed.

Hammerman's face was already the way it would be when he was a man. When Mouse read of boys having to go to work in the coal mines and cotton mills at age twelve and thirteen in the old days, it did not seem possible until he had seen Marv Hammerman.

Hammerman's face did not change expression when he saw Mouse, just sharpened a little. Mouse thought his own face might have been made of thin rubber, it was changing expression so rapidly. His face twisted into shock as he saw Hammerman, then into fear. Then, quickly, awkwardly, Mouse pantomimed that he had forgotten something. He turned and ran back into the school. Once inside, he had run through the halls, down the back stairs, out the side exit and twenty-five blocks out of his way to get home.

To take his mind off Hammerman, he tried to think of another of Ezzie's emergencies. These emergencies were the only things that could make him feel better.

Emergency Seven – Seizure by Gorilla. If this happens, you relax completely and make soothing noises deep in your throat. Ezzie claimed this was foolproof, but Mouse had never been convinced.

'I tell you it's a sure thing, Mouse,' Ezzie had said. 'You make the soothing noises, and he lets you go.'

'I still don't think it would work.'

'All right,' Ezzie had said, 'when a gorilla gets *you*, you scream and kick and holler. When one gets *me*, I'm making soothing noises.' Ezzie had been sensitive about the success of his emergency methods.

Emergency Eight – Attack by Killer Whale. This is one of life's most serious emergencies. When this happens, you swim away from the whale as rapidly as possible. Do not try to get swallowed because, Ezzie said, there isn't as much air in those whales as you'd think. If you do get swallowed by accident, take small measured breaths and try to get coughed out. Then you start swimming away rapidly again.

Mouse passed Margy's apartment he was so busy thinking about the killer whale. Then he turned around. He went up the stairs, entered the apartment and knocked at the first door. When Margy, Mrs. Casino's daughter, opened it, he said, 'I came for Mr. Casino.'

'Oh, yes.' She turned. 'Papa, the Fawley boy's here for you.' She went over and said, 'Papa, you ready to go home?'

Mr. Casino was staring at the television with eyes that seemed to have pulled back into his head a little. He did not look up. She touched his shoulder.

'Papa, you ready to go?' She got him to his feet. He had once been an enormous man but was bent over now so that she could put his overcoat on and button it with ease. 'He's ready, Benjie.'

Mouse was waiting at the door, and she brought Mr. Casino over. She put his hand on Mouse's shoulder, and the two of them went outside and down the stairs. Mr. Casino moved slowly, shifting his weight noticeably with each step, favouring his left leg, rocking back and forth.

Mr. Casino had been like this for as long as Mouse could remember, but Mrs. Casino was always talking about the time, before his illness, when he had been the strongest man in the town. He was so strong, she said, that the cry, 'Get Mr. Casino!' would bring everyone in the neighbourhood running to see what feat of strength he would do this time. His skill as a furniture mover had been such a legend, she said, that people would stand on the sidewalk like it was a parade to watch Mr. Casino lift armchairs over his head as if they were basketballs.

Then came the stroke that would have killed another man. Mr. Casino had lived, but all that was left of his strength was the iron jaw which jutted out from his face. Mouse walked along beside Mr. Casino, keeping his steps in rhythm. He said, 'Mr. Casino, some boys are going to kill me.'

There was no reaction. Mr. Casino's huge hand on Mouse's shoulder did not even tighten in sympathy. It made Mouse sad because he wanted a great reaction. He wanted Mr. Casino's old strength to return, Samson-like. He wanted Mr. Casino to roar with rage, to stretch out his long arms and threaten to pull down whole buildings if those boys were not brought before him.

Mouse said, 'Did you hear me? Some boys are going to—'

Suddenly he heard a shout behind him. He stopped walking, turned and saw Ezzie running towards him. Ezzie was waving his hands in the air, shouting, 'Hammerman! Hammerman!'

Mouse said, 'Wait a minute, Mr. Casino,' in a voice so low it seemed to come from the bottom of a well. He said louder, 'Wait! Stop, Mr. Casino.' Mr. Casino walked a few more steps and then stopped. Mouse ran back towards Ezzie, and then Ezzie grabbed his arm and swung them both around with his momentum.

'Hammerman's coming,' Ezzie gasped.

'What?'

Ezzie pointed behind him. 'Hammerman's coming,' he said. He panted for breath and tried to swallow air into his lungs. 'He's in front of the newsstand, he and the black sweatshirt. I saw them – they were coming this way – and I had to run all the way around to—' He gave up trying to speak, hung his head and gasped.

It seemed to Mouse that while Ezzie was having the most terrible trouble getting breath, he, Mouse, had stopped breathing altogether. Actually, the whole world seemed to have stopped. It had ground down like an enormous, overworked machine. 'In front of Hogan's newsstand?' he asked.

'Yeah.' Ezzie pointed, jabbing his finger in the air. 'Right *there*.'

Mouse said in a rush, 'Look, Ez, could you take Mr. Casino home for me? Just walk with him – that's all you have to do – because if I run I can probably get home before Hammerman sees me.'

'I can't, Mouse, I got to get home myself.' Now Ezzie seemed to have stopped breathing too.

'Ezzie, listen—'

'My dad will kill me, Mouse, you know that.' Ezzie was not as afraid of his father as he pretended, but he *was* afraid of Mr. Casino. He had once come upon Mr. Casino unexpectedly on the landing outside Mouse's apartment. In that dark spot, Mr. Casino had seemed with his huge body and sunken eyes a terrifying figure. Ezzie had gasped and stood there, flattened against the wall, too frightened to raise his voice above a squeak. Even when Mouse had come out and said, 'Oh, that's just Mr. Casino,' Ezzie had still been frightened. 'Oh, yeah,' he had said, '*just* Mr. Casino,' and he had done a Frankenstein-like imitation of him to cover up his fear.

Now he said, 'I got to go. Hurry, and you'll get home, Mouse. You can make it.'

Mouse said, 'Wait a minute, Ezzie. Look, if you'll—'

Ezzie was already running, pointing to his imaginary watch. 'I got to go.'

'Ezzie—'

'I *got* to.'

Ezzie ran backward for a few steps, and then he turned and crossed the street. He waited for a car to pass, then ran faster. Mouse could see from the way Ezzie was running that he was not going to change his mind.

'Come on, Mr. Casino,' he said quickly. He hesitated for a moment, torn between whether he should try to return to Margy's or get home. He put one arm around Mr. Casino's huge waist and pushed him forward. 'Let's go home.' Slowly Mr. Casino began his rocking steps.

Mouse glanced over his shoulder. The sidewalk was empty. 'Let's *go*, Mr. Casino.' He turned and looked back again. 'Let's *go*.'

His head was pounding with fear. He

could not even swallow. He expected his legs to fold up at any moment like the legs of an old card table.

The street was deserted now. That was another thing that frightened him. There was no one who could help him. He glanced back over his shoulder again. And then abruptly he felt that he could not bear the suspense any longer. He knew that Hammerman would be coming around the corner at any second – it was the instinct that comes to the hunted occasionally. He knew that Marv Hammerman was at this moment ready to round the corner of Fourth Street and catch sight of him and Mr. Casino making their endless way home. Then he would be lost. Mr. Casino, too.

He said, 'Come in here, Mr. Casino. Quick!' Mouse went in the first door he came to and found himself in the dark entrance hall of an apartment. He put Mr. Casino back against the wall where the mailboxes were. He said, 'Stand there.' Then he opened the door a crack and looked out.

The street was still empty. Mouse waited at the door with his hands in his jacket pockets. He said without looking around, 'We'll go in just a minute, Mr. Casino. This won't take but a minute.' He opened the door again. There was no one in sight, and he opened the door wider. He stuck his head out this time, and at that moment Marv Hammerman and the boy in the black sweatshirt came around the corner.

Mouse drew back quickly against Mr. Casino, clutching Mr. Casino's coat. He felt Mr. Casino's huge body stirring beneath the cloth and he took his hand. 'We'll go in a minute.' He wondered if Hammerman had seen him glance out the door. If so, all was lost.

Mouse reached around Mr. Casino and tried the door that led to the apartments. As he had feared, it was locked. He and Mr. Casino were trapped in this musty smelly entrance hall. A person could be beaten and left for dead in a hall like this, Mouse thought. No one would even come out of his apartment to see what all the yelling was about.

Mr. Casino took a step towards the front door and Mouse said, 'No, no, Mr. Casino. Wait a minute.' He held Mr. Casino's arm with both hands and drew him back against the mailboxes. Mr. Casino remained beside him for a moment and then made a movement towards the door again.

'Just a minute, Mr. Casino.' Mouse dared not lean forward and look out the door for fear Marv Hammerman would be glancing at the door at the same moment. 'We'll be all right, Mr.

Casino. Don't worry. We're just going to wait here a minute.'

Mr. Casino's overcoat smelled of dry tobacco even though he had not smoked his pipe for years. It was a smell that Mouse associated with his own father. He lost the smell suddenly in the musty odour of the cold hall and he put his face against the overcoat.

Mr. Casino started towards the door again. Mouse said, 'Not yet, Mr. Casino, please.' He held his arm, trying to draw him back. This time Mr. Casino was determined and there was no stopping him. 'Mr. Casino, *please.*' Mouse tugged his arm. '*Please!*' He remembered Mrs. Casino telling about a time during their courtship when ten men had tried to keep Mr. Casino from entering a dance hall where she was doing the polka with another man, and Mr. Casino had toppled all ten men as easily as if they had been bowling pins.

Mr. Casino pushed open the door and started out. Mouse hesitated. He remained against the wall. He was sick. He thought that he shouldn't have eaten those beans for supper. Even four lima beans could be a terrible burden for a stomach under conditions like these.

He swallowed and waited a minute more in the dark hall. He pressed his face against the cold metal mailboxes to see if that would keep him from being sick. Then in a rush he tore himself away from the wall and went out the door after Mr. Casino.

As he came through the door, he had a moment of dizziness. It was as if he had just stepped off one of those rides at the amusement park that Ezzie was so fond of and that made Mouse sick. 'You want to get your money's worth, don't you?' Ezzie would say. Mouse wished that Ezzie was there to stumble around with him, moaning with

57

pleasure at his dizziness. 'Where am I, Mouse, where am I?'

The world was spinning so rapidly that for a minute Mouse couldn't see anything. Marv Hammerman could have been right in front of him, and Mouse wouldn't have been able to see him.

He held onto the banister, leaning on it, and then suddenly everything cleared. Mouse looked up the street and there was Garbage Dog coming toward him with an old Lorna Doone cookie box in his mouth. He looked the other way and there was Mr. Casino making his way back to Margy's. In the distance were two strange boys walking along with a basketball, bouncing it back and forth between them.

Marv Hammerman was nowhere in sight. With an almost sickening sense of relief, Mouse knew that Hammerman had not seen him and had gone on across the street and up Fourth to where he lived.

'Wait a minute, that's the wrong way, Mr. Casino,' he called quickly. 'Wait, Mr. Casino.'

He ran after Mr. Casino and caught up with him just as the two boys stopped bouncing the ball. The boys were looking curiously at Mr. Casino in his long dark overcoat. 'This way,' Mouse said. He turned him around, and with the same slow rocking steps they started for home. 'We'll be all right now.'

Chapter Four

MOUSE entered the apartment and went directly into the hall and sank down on his bed. In the living room his mother was still going through her cosmetic orders. She called, 'Did you get Mr. Casino home all right?'

He said, 'Yes.' He waited, but she did not say anything else. He turned over on his bed and looked at the wall. His heart was still beating so loudly he could hear it. It seemed to him that he had passed through the most dangerous moment of his life. He wanted to call out, 'I was just almost killed in case you are interested,' but he did not. He knew the loud strange way his voice sounded when he was frightened, and he knew that his mother would not be concerned, but only tired, a little disgusted. 'Don't start on that again,' she would say. She never seemed to take danger seriously.

He thought of taking out a pencil, writing on the wall ALIVE AND WELL BY A MIRACLE and drawing an arrow to his collapsed body, but he didn't have the strength to look for a pencil. He lay without moving.

He recalled the time he had had his tonsils out, how lightly his mother had treated that. She had said, 'Look, it's just your tonsils – those little things on the back of your throat. Don't make a big deal out of it.'

But it had been a big deal to him. He could still remember the feeling of being in the hospital, of lying in a strange bed. The only reason he had been able to survive that night at all was because, at the last minute, his father had gone down to the car and brought up his flashlight. It was a big, heavy metal flashlight that his father kept in the car in case of an emergency on the road. His father had brought the flashlight out from under his jacket and quickly poked it under the covers. 'There, now you'll be all right.'

The flashlight *had* made Mouse feel better. The cold metal against his leg had calmed him. And when all the other children had gone to sleep and he alone had lain there awake, he had turned on the flashlight and shone it on the faces of the other children in the ward. He could remember right now the way their faces had looked in the pale circle of light. He thought that if he saw one of those children on the street right now today, he would recognize him and go up and say, 'Hey, weren't you in the hospital one time?'

Marv Hammerman came back into his mind and Mouse shifted onto his other side. He tried to think of something else.

Emergency Nine – Approach of Mad Elephants. When a herd of mad elephants is stampeding in your direction, quickly climb the nearest tall tree and wait. According to Ezzie there was nothing as pleasant as lying coolly on the limb of a huge tree while a herd of mad elephants passed beneath you like a noisy, dusty river.

'Do you have any homework?' his mother called from the living room.

'No.'

'Well, there's a horror movie on channel fifty-three.'

'I might be in in a minute,' he said. He unzipped his jacket and stared up at the ceiling.

Emergency Ten – If attacked by a vampire, make the sign of the cross.

Emergency Eleven – If attacked by a werewolf, draw a six-pointed star and get in it.

The phone rang, and his mother answered it. She came into the hall where he was lying on the day bed. There had been a lot of talk at one time of moving into a larger apartment where he could have a bedroom of his own, but Mouse thought he would feel funny in a bedroom now. The hall with the day bed and the bookcase at the end for his things suited him just fine.

'Your dad wants to talk to you.'

Mouse got up quickly because his father's understanding about the flashlight was still in his mind. Mouse's father had been driving a truck for the last two years, and Mouse hardly ever got to see him. He ran to the phone. 'Hello.' He looked down at the table. On the cover of the telephone book he had written ALL THE NUMBERS IN HERE ARE TO BE DIALLED ON THIS, and then had drawn an arrow to the telephone. 'Hello,' he said again, louder.

'Benjie?'

'Yes, this is me.'

'Well, how are you, son?'

'Fine.' He paused and added with a loud laugh, 'For *now* anyway.' It was his scared voice, but his father did not recognize it over the telephone. Mouse waited for his father to say sympathetically, 'Oh, is there something wrong?'

Suddenly he wanted this more than anything. He began to twist his finger into the telephone cord. He wanted his father to beg. '*Tell me, Benjie*,' he wanted his father to say. 'Whatever the trouble is, I want to know. I demand to know. *Tell* me.'

'Oh, all right,' he would then answer as casually as possible. 'Three boys are going to kill me – Marv Hammerman, Tony Lionni, and a boy in a black sweatshirt.'

His father said, 'I'm in Kentucky and, boy, is it raining. How is it there?'

'Well, the *weather's* all right.'

'Fine, listen, I was just thinking maybe we might do something next weekend. It looks like I'm going to be in town after all.'

Mouse hesitated, holding the phone against his cheek. His mother was not looking at her orders now, but was sitting up straight listening to his conversation. She said, 'Speak up, Benjie, talk to your father. This is long distance.'

'I know, Mom.'

'Well, how about it, Benjie? You want

to do something next weekend?'

'Sure,' Mouse said, 'that would be fine.' Then he laughed again and said, 'If I'm still able to do something.'

'Don't start on that, Benjie,' his mother said in a low voice.

'How does the baseball game sound?' his father said.

'What?'

'The baseball game.'

'Fine, that sounds fine,' Mouse said, looking at his mother.

'Sound excited,' his mother suggested from the sofa. 'He's making a special effort to do this.'

'Yeah, that sounds *very* fine,' he said. He gave up on his father. One by one, the people who could help him were falling away, leaving him to face his trouble alone. It was like one of those western movies.

'And now let me speak to your mom for a minute,' his father was saying.

'Sure.' He held out the phone. 'He wants to speak to you.' His mother came over quickly, and Mouse went back and lay on the day bed. He heard his mother saying in a low voice, 'No, no, there's nothing wrong with him. No, nothing.' There was a pause. Her voice got lower. 'He's just got the idea that some boys are after him, that's all. It's nothing.'

He waited, thinking he might be called back to the telephone. Then he heard his mother say, 'No, we can have supper here. You have to eat out too much. No!' She laughed. 'Besides, I've got a new recipe I want to try – a lady served it at one of my parties.' There was a silence. Then she laughed and said, 'Napoleon's hot dogs.'

Mouse turned over. The covers were twisting beneath him like a rope. He looked at the wall and he remembered another dangerous thing that had happened to him, a second crisis survived, like the tonsils.

In September he had got the idea that he would like to climb up the cliff behind the new shopping centre at Hunter's Square. There was a large rock on top with a button-like rock in the centre, and Mouse wanted to climb up, write PRESS FOR SERVICE and draw an arrow to the button. The idea, once it had entered his mind, would not leave; and finally he had persuaded Ezzie to go over to the shopping centre with him.

Ezzie had not been enthusiastic. As Mouse was purchasing a can of spray paint in the dime store, Ezzie had stood there saying, 'What do you want to do this for, Mouse? That's forty-nine good cents you're wasting!' Ezzie never had any money. His father pretended to be deaf when the word allowance was mentioned.

'It's not a waste.'

'We could buy pretzels with that money. You get three pretzels for thirty-nine cents which would leave a dime for—'

'Ez, I'm going to do it.'

There was a deep sigh from Ezzie at this persistence. He followed Mouse out of the store and spoke only when they were facing the solid wall of the cliff. 'Where is it you're going to write this, Mouse?' he asked scornfully. He already knew because Mouse had told him a dozen times.

'There.'

They looked up together. Mouse was squinting into the sun, but Ezzie's face had a flat look. He said, 'Why can't you just write your name over there under the peace sign like any normal person? That's what I'd do.'

'No.'

'Sometimes you're stupid, Mouse.' Ezzie sat down on the ground. 'Well, go on, get it over with.'

Mouse hated Ezzie to be disgusted with him. He was the only good friend Mouse had ever had. He looked at Ezzie who was staring at his feet. 'All right, Ezzie, I'm going to start now if you want to watch.'

'I've seen disasters before,' Ezzie said in a bored voice.

'Here I go anyway.' Climbing up the cliff was easy at first. A lot of boys had climbed and left footholds, but Mouse went slowly anyway. The can of spray paint was tucked in his belt pressing against his stomach.

The higher he climbed, the harder it got. By the time he reached the halfway mark he was winded, and his arms and legs had started to ache. Every minute began to seem like ten.

'I'm still going,' he called to Ezzie, but Ezzie did not answer. Mouse wanted to look down, but he had had to stop doing that a long time ago because of dizziness. 'I'm still going, Ez.'

He had to find little ways to climb now because there did not seem to be any footholds at all. He used roots and crevices and toeholds, and finally he was there. Gasping from exertion and nervousness he panted out, 'I made it, Ez.' Ezzie did not answer.

Holding onto a root with one hand, Mouse took out the spray can. He shook it and began to write. P. 'How does that look, Ez? Can you read it?' He made an R and an E. He leaned to the side to continue with the two S's and suddenly his foot slipped. It was a terrible sickening sensation.

One minute he was painting an S, the next he was hanging by a root with one knee balanced on a sharp rock. His whole life, it seemed, depended on whether this root was going to hold or not.

'Hey, watch it!' Ezzie called.

Mouse couldn't speak. His leg was digging against the cliff, running as if it were in a race by itself. For a moment, Mouse thought it was all over. His leg started going slower. The root began to pull out of the earth. And then miraculously his other hand found a little ledge and his foot found a rock. The root held; his other foot found a toehold.

Ezzie called, 'Hey, don't do that, will you? It makes me nervous.'

Mouse inched his way back to the ledge. '*You!*' he managed to gasp.

'Yeah, me.'

Mouse clung for a moment. He was so weak he thought he might slip down the cliff like a blob of grease.

Ezzie said, 'You dropped your spray can, did you know it?'

'No.'

'It's busted.'

'Oh.'

'The whole nozzle's gone.' Ezzie shook the can. 'It's full of paint but the nozzle's gone. I told you we should have got pretzels.'

'Well, I might as well come down then.'

Lying on his bed now, Mouse thought that that particular emergency, falling off a cliff, had been avoided by one of those simple survival tricks. Brushes with nature were simple. Emergency Twelve – When you are falling off a cliff, grab a root with one hand, a ledge with another, put your foot on a small rock and then coolly climb down.

His mother came to the doorway and said, 'What are you and your dad going to do next weekend?'

'We're going to the baseball game.'

'Well, that will be nice, won't it?'

'Yes.'

'Your father's making a special effort to get home.'

'I wish he could be home all the time,' Mouse said.

'Well, I do too.' She stood there a minute, looking at him. 'Your father doesn't like this either. It's no fun for him to be driving all the time. Anyway, it won't be for ever.' She waited a minute and then said, 'Well, better put on your pyjamas and get to bed.'

He got up quickly as if he had just been lying there waiting for someone to tell him what to do. He went into the bathroom, took his pyjamas from a hook behind the door and got ready for bed.

He lay there for a while. In the living room, his mother had put out the lights and was watching television. He could see the light flickering as the picture changed. He tried to think of another emergency he could handle.

Emergency Thirteen – Octopus Attack. This was one emergency measure everyone agreed upon – John Wayne, Tarzan, Jungle Jim, everybody. It had worked in every South Sea movie Mouse had ever seen. When attacked by an octopus, you stab the octopus in the eye with the knife you have tucked into the waistband of your bathing suit.

He lay without moving. In the living room, his mother switched channels.

Emergency Fourteen – Parachute Jump. If you are called upon to make an unexpected parachute jump from a plane, you must relax your body completely. Ezzie had learned this from a talk show on television. The natural thing, Ezzie had learned, is for the parachute jumper to start making climbing movements with his arms and legs, trying unconsciously to get back up to the safety of the plane. Ezzie said everybody does this, but what *he* would do would be hold his body in a relaxed position, count to ten, and pull the ripcord.

While Mouse was waiting to think of Emergency Fifteen, he fell asleep.

Chapter Five

MOUSE came slowly down the stairs in the morning. There was a small round hole in the plaster by the front door, and Mouse had once drawn an arrow to the hole and had written DROP COINS HERE BEFORE EXITING. He went out the door, looking down at his feet, taking the steps one at a time. He was trying to be late for school now that his efforts not to go at all had failed.

'Mom, I'm sick, hear? I'm really sick,' he had said at breakfast. He had been sick too. 'I can't even eat, I'm so sick.'

'All right, if you're sick, show me some fever,' his mother had said, getting up from the table and going into the bathroom for the thermometer. 'If you don't have fever, you aren't sick enough to stay home.'

He had sat at the table while she went for the thermometer, thinking of how much he missed his father. Breakfast had been a different meal before his father started driving a truck.

Mouse remembered suddenly the way his father used to tell his dreams at breakfast, fantastic dreams that would have Mouse hanging over his plate, too engrossed to eat.

'Did you dream about the little people last night?' would be the first thing he would say to his father in the mornings. The dreams about the little people had been Mouse's all-time favourites. They all ended with the little people, a hundred and eighteen of them, lifting his father and bearing him down the street with such speed that his father appeared to be on roller skates. His father got out of a lot of tight places that way, and the puzzlement of his father's dream enemies as he slipped past them in this manner never failed to delight Mouse.

Now that Mouse was older and had dreams of his own to remember, he thought that the dreams of the little people were just stories his father had made up to amuse him. Still, he wouldn't mind right now, as big as he was, hearing another of those little people dreams.

His mother returned with the thermometer and he said, 'There are lots of illnesses that you don't have a fever with, Mom. Didn't you ever hear of food poisoning?'

'Put this in your mouth.'

He had known it was hopeless, but he had kept the thermometer in his mouth, rubbing it with his tongue just in case the friction might somehow cause the mercury to rise.

His mother waited by the table. Then she removed the thermometer and looked at it. 'Normal. Get your books and go to school.'

'Mom, I am *sick*.'

'Go.'

Slowly Mouse left the apartment and walked in the direction of school. He knew that he would have to be very late in order to miss Marv Hammerman, because Hammerman never went into the school until the last possible minute. He just lounged outside with his friends.

The street was empty except for two ladies talking, and Garbage Dog who was standing by the ladies looking up at them. There was the faint aroma of bacon grease about one of the ladies. 'Go on,' one of the ladies said, kicking at him.

Garbage Dog moved back a few steps and continued to stand watching them. On his short legs he appeared to be lying down. Mouse remembered that he had once measured Garbage Dog's legs as part of an arithmetic assignment about learning to use the ruler. Each student had had to measure ten things, and the first thing Mouse had measured was Garbage Dog's legs. They were not quite three inches long.

It had been an impressive way to start out the list of things he had measured. Garbage Dog's legs – two and seven-eighths inches.

At least half the people in the class had not believed that figure. 'Hey, no dog's got legs that short,' one boy had cried.

'This one does.'

'Two and seven-eighths inches?'

'Yes, two and seven-eighths inches.'

'That's just *that* long.'

'I know. Listen, I can bring this dog to class if you want me to, Miss Regent. I can catch him and we can—'

'No, Benjie,' Miss Regent had said quickly, 'I don't think that will be necessary. Some dogs do have very short legs.'

'But two and seven-eighths inches!' the boy had cried again, holding up his paper ruler. 'That's just *that* long.'

Mouse knelt and scratched Garbage Dog behind the ears. He must have hit the spot where it really itched, because Garbage Dog leaned back, his nose pointing to the sky, and started making a moaning noise.

'That feel good?' It was surprising, Mouse thought, that a dog like this who had never known soap or flea powder could smell so nice and fresh.

It was a kind of dairy and dry leaves smell. 'There? Is that where it itches?'

The quiet of the street made Mouse think he was late enough. 'I better go.' Still kneeling, he took out his pencil, wrote SCRATCH ME on a smooth spot on the sidewalk and a drew a little arrow to Garbage Dog. Then he rose.

As he walked, Hammerman came back into his mind. It seemed to Mouse that everything, everybody, had suddenly shrunk in importance, making Marv Hammerman a giant. Hammerman towered over the street in Mouse's mind so that the buildings were toys around his ankles, and the pigeons that roosted on the roofs flew around Hammerman's knees.

Mouse walked slower and when he got to the school, it was deserted. The late bell was ringing. Mouse took the steps two at a time and then ran down the hall to his room.

'You're late, Benjie,' Mr. Stein said, looking up at Mouse from his desk.

'Yes, sir, my mom thought I was sick.'

He sat at his desk, pulled off his knitted hat and stuffed it in his pocket. He was taking off his jacket when Dick Fellini nudged him in the back. He turned and Dick said, 'Ezzie wants you.'

Mouse glanced back at Ezzie, and Ezzie's mouth formed the words, 'Did you see Hammerman last night?' Mouse nodded. 'What happened?' Ezzie asked.

Mr. Stein said, 'Ezzie have you got something to share with the class?'

'No, sir.'

'Then why are you talking?'

'I don't know.'

'You don't *know*?'

'No.'

'Then if you don't know, I suggest that you stop,' Mr. Stein said.

'Sure.' Ezzie waited until Mr. Stein was busy with some papers, and then he punched the boy in front of him and whispered, 'Tell Mouse that Hammerman was looking for him this morning. Pass it on.'

Four seats up, Mouse could hear what Ezzie had said perfectly. Then he had to listen to it being passed down the row of seats. To Frankie. To Louise. To Dick Fellini. He waited, and Dick said in his ear, 'Ezzie says Hammerman was looking for you this morning.'

Mouse nodded. He wished suddenly that he could be part of this chain of whisperers. He wished he could nudge the boy in front of him and say, 'Hammerman's looking for Mouse. Pass it on.' What it came down to, he supposed, was that he wished he wasn't Mouse.

'What did you do to Hammerman anyway?' Dick Fellini asked in his ear.

Mouse lifted his shoulders and let them fall.

He felt terrible. He wondered how anybody could feel this sick and not have a fever. It didn't seem possible.

Mr. Stein was saying, 'Let's see now. I had some announcements. Did anybody see a pink mimeographed sheet?'

'Is that it on the floor, Mr. Stein?'

'Yes, thank you, Rose. Now let's see what confusion the office has arranged for us today.' He glanced up and said, 'Yes, Benjie, what is it?'

Mouse cleared his throat and said, 'Could I go get a drink of water?' He paused and then added, 'I don't feel very good.'

Mr. Stein looked at Mouse. Mr. Stein didn't rely on thermometers. Over the years he had developed an eye for the faker. He looked, judged and said, 'I guess so, Benjie.' Mouse got up quickly and started for the door. Then Mr. Stein added, 'Only I wish you kids wouldn't come to school when you're sick.'

'I didn't have any fever.'

'Most people don't early in the morning.'

'Oh.' Mouse wished he had had this piece of information earlier.

'You come to school, infect everyone and go home. *Then* you get the fever. And where does that leave the rest of us?' Mr. Stein had gotten mumps two winters ago from a boy named Beanie Johnson, and Mr. Stein had been cautious ever since.

Wanting to reassure Mr. Stein that this was not a similar case, Mouse said in a low voice, 'I think this is more like food poisoning, Mr. Stein.'

'Well, let's hope so. Go on and get some water and see if that helps.'

Mouse went out into the hall. As he closed the door he heard Ezzie say, 'Could I go get a drink of water too, Mr. Stein?'

Mr. Stein looked him over. 'No.'

Mouse walked on down the hall. When Ezzie was smaller, Mouse remembered that he used to keep a tooth in his pocket for emergencies like this. Then he could always go for a drink. He would hold up the tooth and say, 'My tooth came out. Can I go get a drink, Miss Regent?' It used to work all the time. It was the only good he ever got out of his lost teeth, because Ezzie's parents had never heard of the tooth fairy. They claimed it was something Ezzie had invented to get money out of them.

Ezzie had even made Mouse go home with him once. Mouse had stood there in the kitchen in front of Ezzie's mother, while Ezzie, pink-faced and earnest, had said, 'Go on, Mouse, tell her.

Is there a tooth fairy or not? All I'm asking for is the truth.'

Mouse had waited a moment for Ezzie's mother to look at him, but she continued to baste something in the oven.

'Mrs. Weimer?' She had glanced up at him then, her face red and shiny with heat. 'Mrs. Weimer,' he had said, 'there *is* a tooth fairy.'

'A what?'

Ezzie had shoved him aside. 'A tooth fairy, Mom.'

Mouse had stepped around Ezzie. 'What the tooth fairy does, Mrs. Weimer, is leave money under people's pillows when they lose a tooth.'

Mrs. Weimer finished basting the meat and put it back in the oven.

'Mrs. Weimer,' Mouse had continued, even though the smell of failure was mingled with the odour of meat, 'Mrs. Weimer, *you* are the tooth fairy, you and Mr. Weimer.'

'Did you hear that, Mom?' Ezzie had said. 'Did you hear who the tooth fairy really is?'

'I don't think it's going to work,' Mouse had said under his breath.

'It's *got* to.' If it didn't, Ezzie was not going to be able to go to dawn-to-dusk science-fiction day at the Rialto on Saturday. 'It's *got* to.'

But it hadn't. The next morning when Ezzie looked under his pillow, there was no money. There was only his tooth still wrapped in a little piece of toilet paper.

Mouse walked down to the water fountain and took a few swallows of water. It was warm and tasted of iodine. Ezzie had once said he thought that the teachers were putting a chemical into the water to make them all behave.

Mouse stood at the water fountain. Overhead the hall clock counted out a minute. The school clock didn't just tick like other clocks, it jerked out the minutes. There had never been enough noise in the hall, not even between classes, to drown out the sound of the clock. Mouse waited for another minute to be sounded, and then he turned and went back to his room.

'Do you feel any better, Benjie?' Mr. Stein asked.

'Yes, I'm fine now.' He took out his pencil, drew an arrow to himself and wrote FINE on the pale wood of his desk. Then he rubbed it away with his thumb and waited for Mr. Stein to tell them to take out their English books.

He was still sitting there fifteen minutes later, staring at his desk, when he realized with a start that everyone else had their English books out and open to the story about King Arthur. Mouse looked around in astonishment. Dick Fellini was trying to explain a knight's honour. At the back of the room, Ezzie was swinging his hand in the air like an upside-down pendulum so that he could get Mr. Stein's attention and tell the class the plot of a movie about knights he had seen recently on television. Ezzie got tired of waiting to be called on. 'Mr. Stein! Mr. Stein!'

Mr. Stein ignored him. He said to Dick Fellini, 'Do you think, Dick, that honour and truth and the things the knights stood for have changed, or do you think they still hold true today?'

'Let me think,' Dick said.

Ezzie could wait no longer to join in the discussion. Still waving his hand in the air he made a generous offer. 'Ask me anything you want to about honour, Mr. Stein, and I'll tell you.'

Chapter Six

IT was right after history class when Mouse saw Hammerman for the first time that day. All morning he had been running from one class to another, pushing people aside in his haste, bumping into others, darting around the edge of the hall. The only thought in his mind was getting to the safety of his next class.

'Watch it, Mouse!'

'Look out, Mouse!'

'Quit pushing, Mouse!'

It occurred to him as he ran that there could be no question of how he got his nickname this day. He *was* a mouse. He wished his mother was there to see him because she was always asking, 'Why do they call you Mouse?'

'Because I act like one, I guess,' he had answered, but this hadn't satisfied her.

'Well, tell them to stop.'

'Mom, you don't *tell* people what to call you.'

'A nickname like that can stick with you.'

'I don't care.'

'Well, you will. If you get to be president of a college or a company some day, people will still be calling you Mouse.'

'I don't think you have to worry. I'm not planning to be president of anything.' But the idea had stuck with him. 'I, Mouse Fawley, do hereby swear that as president of this great company . . .'

It did sound bad. 'And now we take great pride in presenting the distinguished and honourable president of our university – Mouse Fawley!' Very bad.

By lunch time Mouse began to think he was going to make it through the day without seeing Hammerman at all. Then after history he came out of class on the run. He was the first person out of the room and he started quickly down the hall. He had been out of his seat so fast that the hall was deserted. Even the library had not started to empty yet. Feeling safe, Mouse had glanced down at his books, which were slipping, and when he looked up he saw Marv Hammerman standing by the door to the boys' rest room. It was as sudden as a feat of magic.

Mouse spun around abruptly. His math class was just down the hall, but he would have to pass Hammerman to get to it. He decided instead on a safer route. He would run down the stairs, cross the first-floor hall and then run up the other stairs to math. He no longer cared how it looked to run like this. He only wanted to avoid a meeting with Hammerman at all costs.

By the time he was coming up the other stairs, the crowd in the hall and on the steps was beginning to thin. Mouse was running. He was dodging the remaining people as if he was playing a strange game. He was almost to the landing when he looked up and saw that Hammerman was waiting at the top of the stairs. While Mouse had been making this long, frenzied run, Hammerman had coolly walked down the hall and waited, catlike, for him.

Mouse stopped. All day he had been hearing the phrase, 'Hammerman's after Mouse,' and now the people on the steps began to walk more slowly, casting glances at them. Mouse knew that the whole school was waiting for the slaughter.

He couldn't run now and so he came up the stairs slowly, pulling himself along with the aid of the banister. He was aware that he was not safe even in the hall. He remembered hearing that one time Hammerman had hit someone in front of the auditorium, and a teacher was standing right there and didn't see it. The boy had been knocked off his feet, Mouse remembered hearing, a huge knot parting his hair, and the teacher had thought the boy had fainted from lack of air.

That's how slick Hammerman was, Mouse thought. It would not have surprised him if Hammerman had leaned over and with the most casual of blows sent Mouse reeling backward down the stairs. Hammerman would be able to do this so skilfully that the few stragglers who saw it would swear that Mouse had tripped. But then, in fear, they would probably do that anyway.

The late bell rang, and Mouse slowly kept coming up the stairs. When he got to the top, all the stragglers were gone except a boy on the landing below who was pretending to straighten his books. Mouse felt that there was nobody in the world but him and Hammerman. He said, 'I'm late for math,' and kept looking at his shoes.

Then he glanced up, squinting at Hammerman, and Hammerman moved his face as if he had chewing gum or a Life Saver in his mouth.

Mouse said, 'Did you say something?'

Hammerman shook his head, and with the sun coming in the window behind him, his hair seemed to fan out like feathers. His face didn't change expression but his eyes were very bright.

Mouse thought that this was because he was doing the one thing he was really good at.

Hammerman's nostrils widened a little, and Mouse wondered if Hammerman could smell fear the way animals could. He had read somewhere that animals become disgusted by the smell of fear and this causes them to attack. Mouse was sure the whole stairway reeked with his fear now. He felt as if he was going to choke on it himself. Emergency Fifteen – When you are afraid, don't let your body know it.

'I really didn't hear what you said, if you said anything,' Mouse said, stuttering a little.

'I'll see you after school.' Hammerman took his finger and touched Mouse on the chest and then passed him and started down the stairs.

'What?' Mouse asked.

Hammerman let the air come out of his nostrils in a sigh of disgust. Still, Mouse knew, a little thing like not having a worthy opponent wasn't going to cause Marv Hammerman to give up the fight.

Without turning around Hammerman said, 'After school.'

Mouse said, 'Oh, sure.'

Hammerman went down the steps so smoothly he might have been sliding. Mouse went to his math class and sat down. He could still feel the place on his chest where Hammerman had touched him. He thought that if he opened his shirt he would be able to see a red dot there, marking the spot.

Across the room Ezzie was waving his arms to get Mouse's attention. Mouse looked and watched Ezzie's mouth form the question, 'Did anything happen with Hammerman?' Mouse nodded. 'What?'

Mouse said, 'I'll tell you later,' beneath his

breath. He started turning through his notebook as if he were searching for an important paper.

A moment passed, and the boy next to Mouse touched his arm. 'Ezzie wants you.'

Mouse nodded but continued looking through his papers. The boy nudged him again and jerked his thumb towards the far side of the room. 'Ezzie.' With a sigh Mouse stopped looking in his notebook for the imaginary paper. He looked at Ezzie.

'What happened?' Ezzie asked again, pouncing on each word. 'What happened with Hammerman?'

The teacher opened her book, looked up at the class and said, 'Ezzie, could I have your attention please?'

Ezzie was beyond hearing the teacher. He leaned over the aisle. *What happened?*

'Ezzie!' the teacher said. Now he heard and

looked up, startled. 'Take your book and go to the board, will you?'

Ezzie stood up quickly, found his book and walked slowly up the aisle, holding the book in one hand. As he passed the teacher's desk he said, 'I didn't have time to study much last night because my sister was sick. She made me put out the light.'

'Put the first problem on the board, please.'

Ezzie picked up the chalk and looked carefully at his book. Mouse also opened his book and tried to concentrate. It was amazing how difficult it was to get your mind *off* something, he thought.

Ezzie put the chalk to his lips. He appeared to be ready to drink a vial of white liquid, perhaps the 'smart' medicine he was always hoping some scientist would discover – one sip and instant smartness. He said regretfully, 'This was the one problem I didn't get, Mrs. Romanoski, I remember now. I got all the others, but this one stumped me.'

'It's exactly like problem two.'

'It is?' His face was blanked by surprise.

'So if you got problem two, then you should be able to do problem one.'

'Yeah, I guess so.'

Mouse tried again to concentrate, but he couldn't. The thought of Marv Hammerman filled his mind completely. He thought that if doctors were running an experiment on his brain, pouring ideas in, the ideas would just flow right out because there was no room left.

Slowly, glancing frequently at the book, Ezzie began to put his problem on the board. Mrs. Romanoski waited a minute and then said, 'Ezzie, this is *not* an addition problem.'

'It isn't?'

'No.'

'Are you kidding me, Mrs. Romanoski?'

'It is *not* addition.'

'Oh.' Quickly Ezzie erased the plus sign with his fingers, leaving a clear round spot on the dusty blackboard. 'Wait a minute.' He hesitated. 'Are we looking at the same problem?'

'Problem one.'

'Yeah,' he said, shaking his head from side to side. 'Problem one.' He paused and then said in an enlightened voice, 'What *page*, Mrs. Romanoski?'

'Page forty.'

'Yeah.' His voice sagged. 'Problem one, page forty.' He took another sip of chalk. 'Wait a minute, let me read this thing again.'

Mouse let his head drop down on his book and felt the cool page against his face. His temperature, he thought now, was beyond being registered, rapidly approaching the point where the body shrivelled like a raisin.

'Benjie, are you all right?' Mrs. Romanoski

asked. He lifted his head and looked at her. 'You don't look well to me.'

'I don't feel good either,' he said.

'Then perhaps you should go to the office.'

He hesitated. 'All right.'

'I'll go with him,' Ezzie offered quickly.

'No, Ezzie, you continue with your problem.'

'But—'

'Ezzie.'

There was a silence as Mouse got up, gathered his books and walked to the door. As he went out into the hall he heard the teacher say, 'All right, Ezzie, it's a multiplication problem.'

'*Multiplication?*'

'Yes.'

'Well, that's what I thought.'

Quickly Mouse started down the deserted stairs to the office.

Chapter Seven

MOUSE was lying on the sofa watching a cartoon. It was the kind of old cartoon that he particularly disliked – the ones in which boxes of soap powder and tubes of toothpaste dance on little legs, but he kept watching. It was four o'clock in the afternoon, and school had been over for thirty minutes. Mouse had been lying on the sofa since then, imagining Marv Hammerman standing outside the school waiting for him. He knew exactly how Hammerman would look – relaxed, watchful, his hair flowing, his hands hooked in his back jeans pockets, his eyes bright, his face expressionless. Mouse had not been able to get that picture out of his mind.

He watched some matches singing, 'I Don't Want to Set the World on Fire' in high voices, and then there was a knock at the door. Mouse got up so quickly that he knocked a glass off onto the floor. He walked silently into the middle of the room to see if the door was locked. It wasn't.

The knock came again. Mouse waited, wondering if he should try to climb out on the fire escape and hide. He imagined the door bursting open and Hammerman standing there, filling the doorway.

There was another knock. 'Hey, Mouse, you in there?' It was Ezzie, and Mouse called quickly, 'Yeah, come on in.' He went back and picked up the glass and the two ice cubes that had spilled onto the rug.

'How are you feeling?' Ezzie asked.

'Oh, all right.'

'Hammerman was looking for you after school.'

Mouse moistened his lips. 'He told me to meet him, but I was sick. They made me go home.'

'The boy in the black sweatshirt – you know which one he is?'

'Yes.'

'Well, he and Hammerman came over to me after school.'

'What did they say?'

'Hammerman just said, "Where's your buddy?"'

'Tell me every word, Ez, don't leave out a thing.'

'That *was* every word. "Where's your buddy?"'

'So what did you say? Did you tell him I had to go home sick?'

'Yeah.'

'And what did he say to that?' Mouse had the briefest hope that his having to go home sick might cause some sympathy from Hammerman.

'He didn't say anything, but the boy in the black sweatshirt said, "Yeah, *scared* sick," and sort of smiled like this.'

'What else?'

'That was the whole conversation, Mouse. First he said, "Where's your buddy?" Then I said, "He had to go home. He was sick." Then the boy in the black sweatshirt – I found out his name is Peachie – said—'

'Never mind. I remember it,' Mouse said quickly.

'Well, you were the one who wanted to hear it.'

'Once. I wanted to hear it *once*.' He sat down on the sofa. On the television screen a bottle of cough syrup was dancing with a bottle of cold tablets, and every time the bottle of cold tablets did a fancy step, the stopper would come off and the tablets would bounce up into the air and then back into the bottle. Mouse said, 'Turn that thing off, will you?'

Ezzie paused in front of the television to imitate the bottle of cold tablets. 'Hey, look at this, Mouse!'

Mouse glanced at him and then back at the table. 'I said to turn that thing off.' Reluctantly Ezzie stopped dancing, turned off the television and Mouse said in a low voice, 'My problem is that I have a *thing* about being hit, I don't know why it is, Ezzie. I just hate to be hit – or hurt in any way really, especially when I know it's coming. I just *hate* to be hurt. It's one of my personal peculiarities, Ez, and somehow I think that makes people *want* to hit me. It's strange.'

'Listen, nobody wants to get clobbered.'

'Not as bad as me.'

'Sure, it's the same with everybody.'

'I just wish you'd been in the hall with me that first day, Ezzie, and seen the look in Hammerman's eyes—' He broke off. He didn't know why he had said that. It was the moment he wanted most to forget. He added quickly, '*Then* you wouldn't be so—'

'Come on and let's play basketball,' Ezzie interrupted.

'I just don't feel like it.' Mouse wanted to get the conversation around to how unfortunate and unfair his plight was.

'Come *on*, will you? You can't ruin your whole life just because of Hammerman. Besides, if he shows up, you can just go in the grocery store and pretend to be buying something.' He paused, then added with a little smile, 'Band-Aids.'

Mouse got slowly to his feet. 'I don't feel like doing anything.' If he had had a pencil handy he would have drawn an arrow to himself and written the words FRAGILE – DO NOT BEND, FOLD OR MUTILATE.

'Come *on*.'

'Oh, all right.' Reluctantly Mouse followed Ezzie out the door, and they went down the stairs together. Once outside Ezzie ran ahead eagerly and turned into the alley by the bakery. 'Come on, will you?' He ran to the paved area behind the store where the basketball hoop had been put up on the back of the grocery.

Ezzie ran over to where Dick Fellini was idly dribbling the ball and shouted, 'Hey, Fellini!' He begged for the ball with his hands, weaving agilely about the pavement, eluding imaginary guards.

'Fellini!' he cried again. He was open now and could make the perfect lay-up shot.

Ezzie had every move of the basketball player down perfectly. He could execute those high jump shots. He could fake, pivot, and go up for a hook shot. He could make the best-looking free throws of anybody. He could dribble so close to the ground the ball seemed to be rolling. The only thing he couldn't do was get the ball in the basket.

He ran up to the net. 'Hey, Fellini, the ball, gimme the ball!'

Fellini fed him the ball, and Ezzie went up in a graceful arc, threw the ball with one hand and watched it bounce off the rim of the basket. Fellini got the ball from the doorway of the grocery store where it had rolled and began dribbling again.

'Hey, Fellini, the ball!' Ezzie spun around now, leaped into the air and caught the ball. Then in a spectacular move he managed to get the ball off before his feet touched the ground. The ball was about a foot short of the basket, and it bounced to where Mouse was standing. Mouse ignored it and let it roll.

Then Mouse walked over and sat down by the grocery. Garbage Dog was there in the doorway, and when he saw Mouse he came over.

'How you doing, boy?' Mouse rubbed Garbage Dog behind the ears. 'How are you today?' Mouse really liked this dog. He had never realized how much he liked him until this moment. He thought that Garbage Dog was the kind of animal that never actually changed in any way, just revealed new aspects of his personality from time to time. Like the event of last summer. Mouse thought about that as he continued to scratch Garbage Dog behind the ears.

Mouse and Ezzie had been patting Garbage

Dog that day – this had been in August – and while they were just sitting there, patting him, Ezzie had noticed that the dog's mouth was slightly open. He had said, 'Hey, Mouse, what's old G. D. got in his mouth?'

Mouse had bent over and looked. Garbage Dog had long hair that hung over his mouth a little. 'I can't see.'

Ezzie had reached out and lifted the dog's lip by this long hair. 'What is it? Can you see now?'

'No.'

'Well, let's get his mouth open. This is driving me crazy.'

They had struggled to open Garbage Dog's mouth, while the dog sat looking beyond them at the back of the dry cleaners.

'Help me, Mouse, you think I can do this all by myself?'

'I'm helping. He doesn't want to open

his mouth though. That's obvious. You can't just *force*—'

'Yes, you can. There's a spot that you press – it's back behind the jaw somewhere – and this spot makes the dog's mouth spring open. I've seen a lady in my apartment give her dog worm pills this way. Wait a minute. This might be it.' Ezzie pressed on both sides of Garbage Dog's face, and abruptly his mouth opened. A small green turtle fell out onto the pavement.

Mouse and Ezzie had looked at it for a moment without speaking. Then Ezzie said in a wondering voice, 'Am I going crazy, or is that a turtle?'

'It's a turtle.'

'But how could that be? Where would you get a turtle around here?'

'Out of somebody's turtle bowl maybe.'

'Let me see that.' Ezzie had picked up the

turtle and looked at it, turning it over in his hand. 'This is a real living turtle.'

'I know.'

'But how could it be? How could such a thing as this be?'

'I don't know.'

'It's like "Twilight Zone", Mouse. Do you understand what has happened? Garbage Dog has come strolling up with a living breathing turtle in his mouth.'

They had sat there with Garbage Dog between them for a long time that afternoon talking about the turtle, about the strangeness of it. Ezzie kept saying over and over, 'It's a living breathing turtle. This turtle is living and breathing!' And Mouse kept saying, 'I know.' Finally they had argued a little about which one of them owned the turtle, and then they had agreed that it belonged to Ezzie because he had noticed it first.

Later that evening Ezzie had sold the turtle to a girl in his apartment building for a quarter. For weeks after that Ezzie never passed Garbage Dog without checking his mouth, the way other people check the coin return slots in telephone booths.

Now Ezzie was guarding Dick Fellini, waving his hands in Fellini's face, trying to knock the ball from his hands. Suddenly Ezzie was successful. He had the ball, bounced it once, whirled out and away from the basket and lifted his arm in a beautiful shot that missed.

Fellini caught the rebound and shot. Then with a forward dart, Ezzie scooped up the ball and dribbled over to Mouse. 'Hey, Mou-sie Boy.' Ezzie threw the ball to Mouse, and Mouse tossed it back without enthusiasm. 'Come on,' Ezzie urged.

'In a minute,' Mouse said. He did not feel like any physical activity. All his strength had to be saved. If he wasted his life force frivolously in games, he thought, there might not be enough.

'Mouse!' Ezzie threw him the ball again. This time Mouse was caught off-guard, thinking about Hammerman, and the ball landed hard in his stomach. He got to his feet quickly, holding the ball against him.

'Watch what you're doing, will you?' he said. He shifted the ball to his hip.

'I'm sorry. I—'

'Yeah, you're *sorry* all right.'

'Aw, come on, Mouse.'

Mouse stood there with the ball, looking at Ezzie as if he were seeing him for the first time. Dick Fellini, who was waiting beneath the basket, came walking over, shaking his hair out of his eyes. He said, 'Hey, what's with Mouse?'

Ezzie said, 'Nothing. Come on, Mouse.'

Mouse hesitated. Ezzie was standing with his

arms held out for the ball. He said again, 'Come on, Mouse, gimme the ball. Let's play.'

Mouse pulled the ball back and fired it at Ezzie. He threw hard, aiming at Ezzie's stomach. He wanted to crumple Ezzie, to drop him to the pavement. 'Take the ball!' he said.

Ezzie drew back instinctively. The ball missed his stomach, struck him on the hand and then bounced over to Dick Fellini. Fellini took the ball, dribbled to the basket and threw it in. He caught the rebound and made another basket.

Ezzie said, 'You didn't have to hit my sore finger,' in a flat, angry voice.

'What sore finger?' Mouse asked.

'That one.'

'Boy, that really is a sore finger, Ezzie. That's some sore finger – a hangnail.'

Ezzie put his finger in his mouth to ease the pain. All the while he was looking at Mouse, and

Mouse was waiting. Then Ezzie took his finger out of his mouth and looked at it.

Mouse thought then that Ezzie was going to say something funny about his finger, to try to make him laugh. Instead Ezzie turned and ran quickly to where Dick Fellini was lining up for a free throw. Ezzie leaped agilely into the air, trying to intercept the ball, and then he watched while Fellini made the rebound.

'Hey, Fellini, gimme the ball,' he cried, spinning around. 'The ball!'

'Yeah, Fellini, give him the ball so he can miss again,' Mouse shouted. He waited to see if Ezzie was going to answer, to swop insults with him. Ezzie ignored him.

Ezzie said, 'Fellini, gimme the ball.'

Mouse turned and walked towards the alley. He glanced back once, saw Ezzie dribbling in the opposite direction and then he kept going.

He walked slowly, kicking a bottle cap ahead of him. To get his mind off how bad he felt, he tried to think of another emergency he could handle. He couldn't think of anything. He went slowly over a list of the world's greatest dangers – tornadoes, earthquakes, tsetse flies, the piranha. Behind him he heard Ezzie cry again, 'Fellini, the ball, gimme the ball.'

He kept going. Cyclones, the coral snake – Then he came to sharks and he stopped.

Emergency Sixteen – Sudden Appearance in Your Swimming Area of Sharks. Ezzie had once read the way to handle that emergency in a comic book. You simply relax your body and play dead. Sharks are bored by dead bodies.

This solution left Mouse dissatisfied. Ezzie had really read that in some comic book, but it was the most unsatisfactory advice Mouse could think of. Play dead! It was impossible.

It seemed to him suddenly that what most emergency measures amounted to was doing whatever was most unnatural. If it was natural to start screaming, survival called for keeping perfectly quiet. If it was natural to run, the best thing to do was to stand still. Whatever was the hardest, that was what you had to do sometimes to survive. The hardest thing of all, it seemed to him, was not running.

He tried to imagine him and Ezzie in the ocean playing dead while the curious sharks swam around them.

'It'll work, it'll work, I tell you,' Ezzie would be muttering out of the side of his mouth. 'It worked for Popeye, didn't it?'

Mouse thought of it a moment longer. He imagined the sharks moving away and he and Ezzie floating alone in the ocean. 'I told you nothing would happen,' Ezzie would say, smiling a little. Somehow this didn't make Mouse feel any better.

Emergency Seventeen – Visit of a Cobra. When this happens, Ezzie said, you stop whatever you are doing at once and you begin to make smooth rhythmic body movements which will hypnotize the cobra.

He remembered that Ezzie had once shown him exactly how these movements should be done. 'Like this, Mouse, like this, see?'

'I don't think movements like that would hypnotize a cobra.'

'Well, I happen to know a boy who hypnotized a cobra in a zoo like this,' Ezzie had said, stopping the movements abruptly. 'And if you don't believe me, his name was Albert Watts.'

Mouse sighed. He kicked the bottle cap into the gutter. Anyway, he thought, life and death struggles with cobras and sharks and lions seemed less likely every day.

He heard a noise behind him, and he looked around and saw Garbage Dog following on his short legs. 'Good boy!' he cried. He had never been so glad to see anyone. 'Come on. You want something to eat? Come to my house.'

At the stairs to the apartment Garbage Dog hesitated, and Mouse drew him quickly forward. 'Come on, boy, food!' Slowly, with Mouse urging him along, Garbage Dog began to take the steps one at a time.

Chapter Eight

GARBAGE Dog had not been inside a house for years. He hesitated at the door, and then when Mouse pushed him, he entered. He walked around the edge of the room, avoiding the carpet, until he came to the kitchen. Then he sat uneasily by the table. There was a little hot air blowing on him from under the refrigerator, and this worried him. He moved over by the sink.

'What do you want to eat?' Mouse asked. 'Bologna sandwich all right?'

Garbage Dog's nose started to run as soon as the refrigerator door was opened. He got up, moved forward and looked into the brightly lit box. He could smell meat loaf and bologna and cheese, and then everything blended into a general food smell which was even better. He waited without moving. His eyes were riveted on the refrigerator.

Mouse gathered up bologna and cheese, shut the refrigerator door with his shoulder and got bread from the counter. 'Here,' he said.

Garbage Dog was accustomed to little titbits – crusts of bread and pieces of broken cookies and the dry ends of ice cream cones. He hardly ever got a whole sandwich. He took it in his mouth and stood for a moment, looking at Mouse. Then he went under the table and began to eat. He finished quickly and came back. He stood looking from Mouse to the refrigerator.

'How about bread with bacon grease on it?' Mouse asked. He broke bread into a small bowl and poured bacon grease over it. He was sprinkling this with grated cheese when his mother came into the apartment.

'Benjie?'

'I'm in here, Mom.' He set the bowl on the floor.

'Well, I hope you aren't eating because—' She broke off. 'What is that dog doing in here?'

'I had to let him come up,' Mouse said. 'He followed me.'

'Well, I don't want dogs in here, you should know that. As soon as he finishes, take him out.'

'*If* he'll go. He follows me every—'

'Out.' She went into the living room and said, 'And don't *you* eat anything, because Mrs.

Casino's giving you supper.'

He followed her quickly into the living room. Behind him came Garbage Dog, sliding a little on his short legs. Garbage Dog stepped on the carpet by accident, and then quickly walked over and stood by the front door, looking worried.

'Where are you going?' Mouse asked his mother.

'I've got a cosmetics party,' she said. His mother went to people's houses and showed cosmetics and people bought them. It occurred to Mouse that he had always wanted to see what went on at one of these parties.

He said quickly, 'I could go with you. I could—'

'You know that's out of the question.'

'I wouldn't be any trouble. Nobody would even know I was there.'

'No.'

'But I *want* to go.'

'I've already told Mrs. Casino you would come. Now, I've got about two seconds to get dressed. Where's my new order book, have you seen it?'

She went into her room, and Mouse walked to the front door where Garbage Dog was waiting. Garbage Dog still looked uneasy.

'Come on, you've got to go,' Mouse said, letting his shoulders slump. Eagerly Garbage Dog went out the door and down the stairs. 'You just have to go, that's all. There's nothing I can do.'

Mouse came slowly back up the stairs as his mother was leaving. He waited on the landing for a moment, watching her go, and then he decided he didn't want to go back in the apartment and be by himself. Sighing, he crossed the landing and knocked at the Casinos' door.

'Mrs. Casino, it's me – Benjie Fawley.'

'Come in, Benjie.' She opened the door. 'Come on in and don't mind me. I'm cooking.'

'I guess I'm early.'

'Well, that's good. You can play checkers with Papa. Come on in. He's so lonely these days. That man—'

Mouse interrupted. 'I'm really not very good at checkers. I've hardly played since fourth grade.'

He suddenly wanted very much to sit in the warm kitchen and watch Mrs. Casino cook. She had a comforting manner about her. If he had said, 'Mrs. Casino, some boys are going to kill me,' she wouldn't have wasted time asking, 'Why?' and 'What did you do?' She would have cried, 'Where are those boys? Show me those boys!' She would have yanked on her man's sweater, taken her broom in hand and gone out into the street to find them. 'Show me those boys!'

He had a brief, pleasant picture of Mrs. Casino cornering Marv Hammerman in the alley and raining blows on him with her broom. 'You (*pow*) ain't (*swat*) touching (*smack*) my (*zonk*) Benjie (*pow, bang, smack, swat, zap*)!' There was nothing comforting about sitting with Mr. Casino. Mouse had already told him about the boys being after him and gotten no reaction at all.

Mouse could see Mr. Casino sitting in the other room. He stood in the doorway with Mrs. Casino. He hesitated.

As he was standing there he thought of something that had happened at school the past week. Mrs. Tennent had brought movies of her Christmas vacation to school and had shown them to all her classes. And when she had shown everything that had happened to her and her sister in Mexico, then she reversed the film and they got to see everything happen in reverse.

They got to see Mrs. Tennent walking backward into the hotel and into the bullfight. They got to see her sister walking backward through a market place. They got to see a funny looking taxi driving backward, and people eating backward, and a man diving backward up onto a high cliff. They had all laughed because there was something about people walking backward in that bright, skilful, cheerful way that was funny.

Suddenly that was what Mouse wanted to happen now. He wanted to walk backward out of the Casinos' apartment. He wanted to walk backward to the basketball court, and then to school, reversing everything he had done in a bright, cheerful way. He wanted to move backward through Thursday too, and he especially wanted to walk all the way back to when he had come out of history class and paused by the prehistoric man chart. He wanted to stop everything right there. He would have paused a second, and in that second he would not have lifted his hand to write Marv Hammerman's name. Then the world could go forward again.

He felt Mrs. Casino urging him into the room. He said reluctantly, 'I haven't played checkers in years. I'm not sure I even remember how.'

'You're good enough. Go on.' Mrs. Casino took him firmly by the shoulders and pushed him into the room where Mr. Casino was sitting by the window. 'Papa's just learning checkers over again anyway,' she said.

Mouse crossed the room, dragging his feet. He said, 'Hi, Mr. Casino,' in a low, unenthusiastic voice because he wanted to be *with* somebody. He was lonely. I, Mouse Fawley, do hereby swear that I feel very lonely. He thought he would have to make a declaration of it to make people understand. 'How are you, Mr. Casino?' he asked in the same flat voice.

'He's fine, aren't you, Papa?' Mrs. Casino said. She patted Mr. Casino on the shoulders as she passed behind his chair. Mouse sat down. Mr. Casino was in an armchair, and the bottom had sunk so low that Mouse in his straight chair was the taller of the two.

'Here you go.' Mrs. Casino brought out the checkers, the oldest set Mouse had ever seen, and set it on the table. The black and red board had been worn white where the checkers had been moved across it. When she put the set down, Mr. Casino reached out slowly with one enormous hand. His fingers were trembling a little, as if the distance from the armrest of his chair to the box of checkers was long and hazardous.

'I'll set these up,' Mouse said. 'I can do it better.' Quickly, efficiently, he put the checkers in the squares, his and Mr. Casino's. Then he leaned back in his chair. 'Go ahead, Mr. Casino.' He could hear the impatience in his own voice.

He glanced up at Mrs. Casino, who was still standing by the door, drying her already dry hands on her apron. Then quickly Mouse looked back at the checkerboard because he had seen something in Mrs. Casino's eyes. It was just a flash of something, a cloud over the sun, a sadness, and it bothered him.

She said, 'He's supposed to use his left hand as much as possible.'

'Oh,' Mouse said. He wanted to explain that the reason he was acting this way was because he had the impossible burden of being chased by Marv Hammerman. He wanted Mrs. Casino's sympathy. 'Mrs. Casino,' he wanted to say, 'if you only knew what it's like to have Marv Hammerman out to get you.'

He felt tears stinging his eyes, and he knew he was not going to tell Mrs. Casino, and that he was not going to tell anybody else either. 'Your move,' he said loudly to Mr. Casino. He shifted in his chair and then abruptly he slumped.

He had suddenly thought back to that moment outside history class when he had turned and looked around and seen Hammerman. That first moment – it was what had been troubling him all along.

It wasn't entirely clear. It was as if a fog had filled the hall that day, making everything hazy. Still Mouse could remember the way Hammerman's eyes had looked in that first unguarded moment. There hadn't been enough fog to blot that out. Mouse thought again about that moment in the hall. It had been flitting in and out of his mind like a moth for two days. Now he made himself think about it.

He sank lower in his chair, because he knew now what troubled him. He had felt somehow close to Hammerman in that first terrible moment. He had known how Hammerman felt. It had been the same way he had felt when everyone first started calling him Mouse. They had been united for a moment, Mouse and Neanderthal man.

He said in a low voice, 'You can have first move, Mr. Casino.'

Mr. Casino sat for a moment and then made a gesture with his fingers as if he was flicking a fly off the armrest.

Mrs. Casino said, 'He wants you to go first, Benjie.' She was still patting the backs of her dry hands on her apron.

'Oh, sure.' He looked at the board as if the decision was one of the most important of his life. The checkers were thin and wooden and darker in the centre from the sweat of people's fingers. They were clear for a moment and then they blurred a little. Mouse reached out and pushed one forward before they got so blurred he couldn't find them.

He leaned back in his chair. The late afternoon sun was coming in the window, and the dust in the sunlight gave him a sad, old-timey feeling. He thought that if he closed his eyes, he would not be able to tell even what century he was in. It could be a hundred years ago and he could be sitting here in an old-timey suit with knickers and a tie. It could be a thousand years ago. It was that kind of timeless feeling.

Some things, he thought as he stared down at the checkerboard, just don't change. He remembered how he used to enjoy looking through books that showed the old and the new – the Wright Brothers' glider opposite a jet plane, or an old Victrola opposite a hi-fi set. Looking at pictures like that always made him feel superior, as if he had advanced in the same way as the machines. He felt different now. He thought of all the people who had ever lived as being run through by a single thread, like beads.

'Well, I'll get back to my cooking, if you don't need me,' Mrs. Casino said.

'No, we'll be fine.'

He looked at Mr. Casino who was reaching out slowly. He was still a large man, but he had once been enormous, and everything he was wearing was too big for him. The cuffs of his shirt came down over his speckled hands. The cotton pants were gathered in at the waist with his belt. Mouse waited, watching sadly, while Mr. Casino pushed one of his checkers forward with a trembling hand

Mouse said, 'My turn?' He bent forward over the board.

In the kitchen, Mrs. Casino started to sing. Outside two men were arguing about baseball.

A bus passed. Mrs. Casino started on a western song. Mouse tried not to think of anything but the checker game. He said self-consciously, 'Oh, I've got a jump.' He took it and leaned back in his chair.

It was a long, slow game, the first game Mouse had ever played in which it didn't seem important who the winner was, or rather a game in which both players were winners.

Mouse said, 'Do you want to play again?' He waited a minute, and then he pushed all the checkers across to Mr. Casino and said gently, 'You set them up this time, will you?'

Chapter Nine

SATURDAY was warm and bright, the first pretty Saturday they had had since Christmas. Mouse, lying on his bed in the hall, could tell it was sunny just from the brightness of the normally dark hall.

'Mom!' he called, not knowing what time it was and whether she had gone out to deliver cosmetics yet. 'Mom!' There was no answer. There used to be a boy who lived in the apartment next door when Mouse was little, and every time Mouse would call, 'Mommie!' the boy would answer, 'Whatie?' in a high false voice.

Mouse got out of bed slowly, in stages. He sat on the edge of the bed, leaned forward, looked at his feet, straightened, and then continued to stand by the bed for a moment. Then abruptly he dressed, went into the kitchen and looked at the boxes of cereal on the shelf. He tore open a box of Sugar Pops. He waited, looking at the cereal, and then refolded the box and put it back. He went into the living room, and out of habit he switched on the television. Superman was on the screen, flying over the city in his suit and cape. Mouse watched for a moment and then turned off the television. Superman might be faster than a speeding bullet and able to leap tall buildings with a single bound, Mouse thought, but even Superman couldn't keep himself from being tuned down to a small white dot.

Mouse got his jacket from the chair by the door.

Even though he knew it was going to be warm outside, he put on his jacket and zipped it up. Then he left the apartment.

The street and the sidewalks were crowded. Some girls were roller skating, and it was the first time Mouse had seen that this year. Usually he and Ezzie liked to sit on the steps and watch the girls, calling out things like, 'Congratulations,' when they slipped. This would have been a good time to sit and yell comments of this nature because the girls had lost their talent for skating over the winter.

'Help me,' the biggest girl was yelling. 'Don't let me fall.' While she was screaming, the two smaller girls, sisters in matching sweaters, began to lose their balance. 'Help me,' the big girl cried. The two sisters were now on their knees, still holding the big girl up. 'Help!' the big girl cried and then she too went down on the sidewalk.

'Yeah for Louise!' Ezzie would have cried in delight. He would have nudged Mouse as the girls struggled to their feet, anticipating more fun. 'Get this, Mouse. Keep your eye on Louise. She's the one to watch.'

Mouse passed them without comment. Louise was still sitting on the sidewalk saying, 'I think I broke something. No fooling, I think I broke something.'

Mouse kept walking down the crowded sidewalk. He knew a lot of these people, but nobody seemed to be speaking to him today. It was as if everybody in the world knew what he was going to do, and everybody knew that if they gave him any sympathy at all, if they even patted his shoulder or took his hand, he would not be able to do it. He would just fold up on the sidewalk, curled forward like a shrimp.

He crossed the street, touching both feet on the old trolley tracks because this was supposed to bring luck, and he stepped up on the sidewalk in front of the laundry. He thought that he could walk down this street blindfolded and know right where he was. The odours that came out of the different doors told him what to expect, what cracks there were in the sidewalk, who would be standing in the doorways. He turned the corner, passed the old movie theatre, the Rialto. He smelled the old musty smell. Then he stopped thinking of anything except the fact that he was now on Marv Hammerman's street.

A bus passed him, stopped to pick up an old

woman with a folded shopping bag under her arm and then moved on. Mouse had started to sweat. It wasn't that warm a day, not even with his jacket zipped up, but sweat was running down his sides beneath his shirt in a way it had never done before. At the same time his throat had gone completely dry, and the two conditions seemed somehow connected.

He saw a boy who had been in his school last year and he asked, 'Have you seen Marv Hammerman?' His voice had the crackling dry sound of old leaves. He turned his head away and coughed.

'Not this morning.'

'Doesn't he live around here?'

'He lives right over there,' the boy said. 'Lots of times he's down at Stumpy's.'

'Oh.'

'If I see him I'll tell him you're looking for him.'

'I'm Mouse Fawley,' he said, looking at the boy, and the boy said, 'I know.'

Mouse glanced at his watch. It was 9:31. Slowly he walked the half block to Stumpy's, which was a pizza place that had pinball machines. The entrance was below street level, and Mouse stopped and looked inside for a moment. He couldn't see anything at first because his eyes were still accustomed to the bright light outside, but he could hear the sharp mechanical sounds of the pinball machines, the bells, the clicks, the machine-gun bursts of points being scored. He went down the steps.

'Is Marv Hammerman here?' he asked, squinting up at the man behind the counter. The man was putting packs of gum in a display stand.

He glanced at Mouse and kept on straightening the gum.

'No, he hasn't been in. Hey, Steve, where's Hammerman?'

The man and Mouse waited while Steve's ball travelled down through the bright maze of the pinball machine. Steve urged the ball into the holes with gentle leaning movements of his body. When it was over he said, 'He may be in later.'

'He may be in later,' the man told Mouse.

'Thanks.' Mouse turned and walked out of Stumpy's. He lifted the cuff of his jacket and checked his watch again. It was 9:36. Slowly he began to walk up the sidewalk. This was the one thing he hadn't thought of – that he wouldn't be able to find Hammerman. He walked two more blocks, turned around and came up the other side of the street.

He thought he would not be able to bear the tension if Hammerman did not appear soon. He crossed in front of Stumpy's and started down the street again, moving a little faster. He thought he had been walking for hours. Where could Hammerman be? He looked at his watch again. It was 9:55.

The sunlight seemed blinding now, and Mouse wanted to dim it so that whatever was going to happen would not be lit up for everyone to see. He walked to the end of the block and squinted down at his watch. It was 9:57. He paused in front of the barber shop to wind his watch and found that it was already wound tightly. He could not remember winding it, but it was that strange kind of day when watches could wind themselves and a minute could become an hour and the sun could shine on one single person like a spotlight.

He started walking. He walked in the same quick way, and he was almost back to the old Rialto theatre when he saw Marv Hammerman coming towards him. Hammerman was with the boy in the black sweatshirt, and both of them were walking quickly as if they had heard Mouse was waiting. The boy in the black sweatshirt was smiling a little.

When Mouse saw them, his walking suddenly became harder. His shoes seemed to stick to the sidewalk, and his legs got heavy. He felt as if he were walking under water. He pulled down his jacket, smoothed his hair, hitched up his pants, kept his hands busy in order to keep attention from his slow heavy feet. He pulled at his ear lobe, wiped his nose, zipped his jacket higher. Foolishly he thought of the hundred and eighteen little people of his father's dreams. He wished they would appear, lift him and carry him away. 'So long, Hammerman,' he would cry as they hurried him to safety.

Mouse kept walking, and the three of them met in front of the Rialto by the boarded-up booth where Mouse used to buy tickets to the Saturday science-fiction specials.

Mouse finished working the zipper on his jacket and pulled his cuffs down. He said to Hammerman, 'I was sick yesterday and I had to go home, but I'm here now.'

It came out in a rush. Mouse hoped that he hadn't said it so quickly that Hammerman didn't hear it. It was important that this one thing be said while he was still able to talk.

'He still looks a little sick to me, don't he to you?' the boy in the black sweatshirt said, smiling. 'Course he looks better than he's *gonna* look.'

Mouse didn't say anything. He was trying

to steel himself for the battle. The only thing he knew about fighting, he realized now, was that if you put your thumbs inside your fists and hit somebody hard with your hand like that, you could break your thumb. He rearranged his hands which he had instinctively folded with the thumbs inside.

He cleared his throat, wondering if he was supposed to say something else. He had had so little experience in fighting that he did not know how a fight of this kind, an arranged fight, would actually start. He remembered seeing a fist fight in an old silent movie on television one time, and the opponents had lifted their fists at the same moment, in the same position, and had circled each other in a set pattern. Still he couldn't imagine this fight starting, not in that way or any other. He could only imagine the ending.

The boy in the black sweatshirt jerked his

head at Hammerman. He said to Mouse, 'He don't like anybody writing things about him.'

Mouse was so nervous he thought perhaps the boy had been talking to him for hours. He wasn't certain of anything. He said quickly, 'I know.'

The boy in the black sweatshirt nodded at Hammerman again. He said, 'He wants you to know real good.'

The sun went behind a cloud, and it was suddenly dim beneath the marquee. Mouse couldn't see for a minute. He had been looking at the boy in the sweatshirt while he was talking, and now the boy was silent. All Mouse could see was the whiteness of his smile.

Mouse looked back at Hammerman. For a moment he couldn't see him clearly either. Hammerman's face was a pale circle in the darkness, like the children's faces in the hospital ward, lit up by the light from Mouse's flashlight.

Then, abruptly, everything snapped into focus. Hammerman's face was so clear there seemed to be nothing between Mouse and Hammerman, not even air. They could have been up in that high altitude area where the air thins and even distant points come into focus.

Hammerman hadn't made a move that Mouse could see. He was still standing with his hands at his sides, his feet apart. But his body had lost its relaxed look and was ready in a way that Mouse's body would never be.

Mouse raised his fists. His thumbs were carefully outside, pointing upward so that he appeared to be handling invisible controls of some sort. Then he saw Hammerman's fist coming toward him, the knuckles like pale pecans, and at the same time Mouse saw Hammerman's eyes, pale also but very bright. Then Hammerman's fist slammed into his stomach.

Mouse doubled over and staggered backward a few steps. He thought for a moment that he was going to fall to the ground, just sit down like a baby who has lost his balance. He didn't, and after a second he straightened and came towards Hammerman. He threw out his right hand.

He didn't see Hammerman's fist this time, just felt it in the stomach again. It was so hard that Mouse made a strangled noise. If he had eaten breakfast, there would have been Sugar Pops all over the sidewalk from that blow.

Choking, coughing, he staggered all the way back and hit against the side of the theatre where pictures of man-made monsters used to be posted. He stayed there a minute, bent over his stomach, waiting for his strength to return. He could almost feel the old favourites – Gorgo, Mothra, Godzilla – waiting behind him. He tried to pull himself forward. He felt for a minute that he had become glued to the theatre, plastered there like the pictured monsters. Then he came free and took three heavy steps forward to where Hammerman was waiting. Gorgo had walked like this. Mouse thought of how Gorgo's feet had crushed whole buildings with these same heavy steps. His own feet could barely lift the weight of a pair of tennis shoes.

Mouse's hands were up. He threw the invisible controls forward and hit nothing. Then he felt a sharp stinging blow on his breastbone. He hadn't seen that one coming either. He put out his fists, to ward off blows again rather than to land them, and then Hammerman's fist was in his face. It landed somehow on his nose and mouth at the same time. Then there was another blow directly on his nose.

Mouse's nose began to gush blood. The blood seemed to be coming from everywhere, not just the nose, and Mouse wiped his face with one hand. Quickly, anxiously he got his hands back in position. He threw the right control forward.

Suddenly he couldn't see. He wiped his hand over his eyes, then wiped his nose and got set. He was leaning forward now, pressing his knees together to steady them. The blood from his nose was splattering on the sidewalk.

He waited, wondering how long he could continue to hold this position. Then he heard Hammerman say, 'You had enough?'

'No, he hasn't had enough,' the boy in the black sweatshirt said. 'He's still standing.'

Hammerman said again, 'You had enough?'

Hammerman's voice seemed to be coming from somewhere far away, but the voice wasn't asking the right question, Mouse thought. It seemed simple suddenly. He saw it now as an old-fashioned matter of honour. He, Mouse, had dishonoured Marv Hammerman; and now Hammerman had to be the one to say when his honour was restored. It was one of those things that doesn't become absolutely clear until the last minute and then becomes so clear it dazzles the mind.

Mouse could hear Dick Fellini's voice explaining honour and knighthood to the English class. He could hear Ezzie saying, 'Ask me anything you want to about honour, Mr. Stein, and I'll tell you.' It was an odd thing but he, Mouse, who had felt honour, who had been run through with it like a sword, couldn't say a word about it.

He looked at Hammerman, squinting at him, and said, 'If you have.'

'If *he* has!' the boy in the black sweatshirt cried. 'Man, he can keep going like this all morning.'

There was a long pause, and Mouse suddenly

feared he was going to start crying. He couldn't understand why he should want to cry now when it was almost over. The worst thing that could happen now was the big final blow, the knock-out punch that would leave him unconscious in the shadow of the Rialto. He could even take that if only he did not start crying.

Hammerman lifted one hand and opened it a little as if he were releasing something. It was a strange gesture, and it seemed to Mouse the kind of gesture a dancer might try to make, or a painter might try to put in a picture. He imagined a small statue, bronze, on a round pedestal, of Marv Hammerman with his partially raised open hand.

Hammerman said, 'Go on.'

'What?'

'Go on.'

Mouse wiped his nose with the back of his hand and said, 'Thank you.'

The boy in the black sweatshirt leaned back and hollered, 'Whoooo-eeee! You welcome.'

Mouse passed them, holding his hand over his nose. The boy in the sweatshirt laughed again. It was a loud explosive laugh, and the boy spun around to watch Mouse walk away.

'Whooo-eeee!' he said. 'You are most certainly welcome. Come around anytime.'

Mouse turned the corner and kept walking. Tears were in his eyes now, and he could not see where he was going. It was, he thought, the gesture that had weakened him. The careless ease of that opened hand – Mouse couldn't seem to get that out of his mind.

He made his way down the sidewalk with his eyes closed. He thought suddenly that if he could see where he was going it would probably not be down Fourth Street at all. He was probably walking across some dusty foreign field. If he could look up, he would not see the tops of buildings, the flat blue sky with a jet trail drawn across it. He would see gold and scarlet tournament flags snapping in the wind. There would be plumes and trumpets and horses in bright trappings. Honour would be a simple thing again and so vital that people would talk of it wherever they went.

He felt as if a vanished age had risen up like a huge wave and washed over him. Then he smelled a dry starchy smell and knew he was passing the laundry. He stopped and wiped his hand across his eyes to clear them. He stepped against the wall and then opened the door into an apartment building where he didn't know anybody. He sank down on the steps against the wall.

With a sigh he hung his head and pinched his nose shut. His nose was still bleeding. He saw that now. He noticed the other damage. His upper lip was bleeding and starting to swell. His stomach hurt so bad it might be weeks before it would accept food again. He couldn't bend over any further without feeling the pain in his breastbone. He looked at his watch. It was 10:13.

Well, he thought wryly, at least I didn't break my thumbs.

Chapter Ten

A lady from the lower apartment saw him when she came out to get the mail, leaned over him and asked, 'Are you all right?' She was a big woman. Mouse couldn't see her right then, but he could feel the solidness of her presence.

He nodded. He tried to get up, thinking she wanted him to get out of the hallway. Still holding his hand over his nose, he managed to get to his feet. She said, 'You come on in. Come on now.'

She pulled him forward with her strong arms and led him into her kitchen. 'What happened to you, huh?' she asked as she was wringing out a cloth at the sink. He just shook his head. 'Probably a fight – is that what it was – a fight?' He nodded. 'Either that or you got hit by a freight train. You kids.'

As she came over to where he was sitting, he looked up and was surprised to see that she was a small woman, dark and quick moving. She had a gypsy face. She said, 'You kids never learn. There's a better way to settle things than with your fists, you know that? A clever person never has to feel one single blow his whole life. Let me see your hands. I can't tell what part of you is hurt the worst.'

He held up his hands, bloody but unscarred.

They were hands that hadn't landed a single blow. The woman wiped them clean, finger by finger, the way his mother used to wash his hands when he was little.

'Fighting is not the answer,' she said.

'I know,' he said, able to speak at last. 'Only it wasn't a real fight.'

'Then I'd hate to see you after a real one,' she snapped. She looked at his cleaned hands. She turned them over. 'I bet the other kid didn't get a scratch on him.'

'No.'

'You can't win.'

'I know.'

'Well, at least you've learned that.' Continuing to babble about the dangers of fighting, she stopped his nose from bleeding, gave him a piece of ice to put on his upper lip, washed his face and even, in her concern, wet his hair and combed it. She parted his hair on the wrong side and combed it straight across his forehead. This, plus the swollen lip, made his face look strange reflected in the window over the sink.

'Now, you go right home and lie down, you hear me? Don't let that bleeding start up again, and if it does, you put wadded paper up under your lip like I showed you.'

'Yes, and thank you.'

'And don't fight any more.'

'I won't.' He tried to smile. 'If I can possibly help it.'

'You kids.'

He went outside and for the first time he knew what real relief was. It was a relief so great that the whole world looked different to him, cleaner and sharper. He had not even felt this way when he got out of the hospital after losing his tonsils. It was the kind of light feeling that might come with a lessening of the pull of gravity. He felt that if he wanted to, he could actually float up through the buildings. He imagined himself rising, moving slowly and easily, waving to the startled people in the windows, smiling to them. His body was the lightest, most unburdened thing in the world. Strings would be required in a minute to hold him to the ground.

He walked slowly back to his street, holding the ice cube, which the lady had wrapped in a little square of cloth, against his lip.

As he rounded the corner, he saw Ezzie and Dick Fellini and Dutch Richards standing by the mailbox. Ezzie had his back to Mouse. He was saying to Dutch, 'Aw, come on, gimme the ball. Don't you want to see me do the trick?'

'Frankly, no.'

'Come on, Dutch. If *I* had a new ball and *you* wanted to do a trick with it, I'd—'

Mouse came up and lowered his ice cube. He said, 'Well, I fought Hammerman.'

Dutch stopped bouncing the ball and Ezzie spun around, his trick forgotten. 'You what? You fought Hammerman?' Ezzie asked incredulously.

Mouse nodded.

Ezzie straightened. '*You* fought Hammerman?'

'Yes.'

Mouse knew that Ezzie had had a secret fear that he, as Mouse's best friend, might be called on to participate in the fight. Mouse knew Ezzie was especially afraid that he might have to take on Peachie, the boy in the black sweatshirt. Now it was hard for Ezzie to believe that this danger had passed.

'Where was this fight?' Ezzie asked. 'What happened? Come on, tell me about it.'

'Well, it was in front of the Rialto,' Mouse said. His swollen lip made his voice sound strange, or perhaps it was the strangeness of what he was saying. He stopped and put the ice cube back against his lip.

The Saturday traffic seemed loud in the street. Two boys on motorcycles passed. Ezzie glanced impatiently at them for interrupting and then prompted eagerly, 'So? Go on.'

'Well, I went over to the Rialto looking for Hammerman and—'

'You went looking for *him?*' Ezzie asked.

'Let him tell it, Ezzie,' Dutch said.

'Well, I went over there looking for him,' Mouse continued, 'and we met in front of the Rialto and had a short fight and now it's over.' Mouse thought that those were the most comforting words he had ever heard.

'How short was the fight?' Ezzie asked.

'I mean, in blows. How many blows, Mouse, do you remember, or was it so many that you couldn't—'

'Five,' Mouse said.

'Five!' The hush of Ezzie's voice made five the most important number there was.

'Two in the stomach, one on the breastbone, right about there.' He put his hand over the exact spot. 'Two on the face.' There was no need to point out where those blows had landed.

'You took all those blows?'

Mouse nodded.

'Did you fall down, or what?'

'No, I didn't fall. Well,' he said truthfully, 'I would have fallen if the Rialto theatre hadn't been there, and I staggered around. But I never actually went down.'

Ezzie and Dutch and Dick were looking at him. It was a strange sensation for a minute. It was as if they were not looking at him at all, but at what was going on inside him. They had all four wanted X-ray eyes at one time or another, and now Mouse suddenly had the feeling that the other three had got them. He shrugged self-consciously and said, 'Well, I better go get another ice cube. This one's about gone.'

He started walking, and Ezzie left the others and followed him. He said, 'Listen, I want to hear some more about this fight. What was it really like? I mean, did he say anything, or what? You haven't told me *anything*.'

Mouse turned and looked at Ezzie, squinting in the sunlight. He wet his swollen lip with his tongue and said, 'It was just sort of an honourable thing, Ezzie.'

'A what?'

'An honourable thing.'

'Hammerman? Honourable?'

Mouse nodded. He knew that he was not going to be able to explain it to Ezzie. He wasn't even sure he understood it himself now. But at the moment when he and Marv Hammerman had met in front of the Rialto, it had been clearly and simply a matter of honour.

He wanted to explain. He said, 'Hammerman's not like I thought, Ezzie, that's all I'm trying to say.'

'Are we talking about the same Hammerman?' Ezzie's face had gotten pinker with his puzzlement.

Mouse nodded. 'Marv Hammerman.' He looked down at his tennis shoes which were splattered with blood. He couldn't even see where he had written AIR VENT now. Still looking at his shoes he said, 'I don't even know what Hammerman *is* like. It's strange, Ezzie, I can't explain it in words.'

'Quit fooling now! What happened? How bad was it?' Ezzie threw out his hands in an old gesture of agitation he saw his grandfather use daily. 'Tell me.'

'Well,' Mouse began and then he trailed off. He tried to think of something to tell Ezzie, but he couldn't. He knew how Ezzie felt, cheated at not knowing the details of the ending. He had felt that way one time when he had been watching a television show. Right at the most exciting part a news bulletin about a hijacked airplane had come on, and Mouse never got to see how the story came out. His mother had said, 'Well, you know the dog rescued the boy. Even I can tell you that.'

'Yes,' he had said, 'but I wanted to see it happen.'

Mouse tried to smile with his swollen lip. He shrugged his shoulders. He said, 'Well,

Ezzie, he could have made it a lot worse.'

Ezzie could not understand what was happening, but for some reason, even though Mouse was no longer a tragic figure, no longer marked by destiny, he had not shrunk back to his normal size like Mr. Stein. Even standing there with a bloody jacket and a swollen lip and wet hair that still had the comb marks in it, Mouse seemed bigger. It was such a strong impression that Ezzie wondered if Mouse had actually gotten taller. He wanted to stand back to back with Mouse in front of a mirror and measure.

Mouse started slowly up the steps. Despite the light feeling of his body, his legs weren't working as well as usual.

Ezzie said quickly, 'I'll get an ice cube for you.'

'I'm all right, Ez, I can—'

'No, I'll get it. I want to.'

Ezzie went up the stairs, taking them two at a time. Mouse waited at the bottom, resting his weight on the metal banister. He felt strange. It wasn't the swollen lip or the new part in his hair or the lightness of his body. He had sometimes wished in the past two days that he wasn't himself, and it seemed now that this wish had come true. He almost had to remind himself who he was. I, Benjie Fawley, am alive and well. He let the air out of his lungs in a long sigh. I, Benjie Fawley, have survived.

Dick Fellini called, 'Hey, Benjie, you guys want to play ball?' Fellini was bouncing the basketball, twisting it in such a way that it came back to him as it bounced.

He said, 'Sure,' even though he was not sure his legs were going to cooperate in the plan.

'Well, come on then.'

'I'll wait for Ezzie.'

Dutch and Dick Fellini waved and started down the sidewalk. Mouse waited by the stairs. 'Ez, come on,' he called after a moment.

Ezzie appeared at the window. 'Hey, can I have a bologna sandwich?'

'Yeah, if you'll come on.'

'You want one?'

'No.' He realized suddenly he was hungry after all, and he called out, 'Yeah, Ezzie, I want one.'

Ezzie came back to the window. 'Mustard and relish? And there's some lettuce in a plastic bag and a couple of okra pickles.'

'I don't care, Ezzie, just make it and come on, will you?'

'I'm *coming*, only if you're going to make a sandwich, then you might as well make a *sandwich*.'

Mouse waited, and after a minute Ezzie came

out of the apartment with the sandwiches. 'The ice cube's in my pocket,' he said. Mouse fished the ice cube out of Ezzie's shirt pocket, brushed the lint off and twisted it into the square of cloth. Then he took his sandwich and said, 'Let's go.'

'Right.'

As they walked down the street, Ezzie took a bite of his sandwich, then turned it around to make sure the okra pickles weren't going to fall out. He shook his head and said, 'And you fought Hammerman.'

A passing bus blocked out the answer, which was, 'Well, not really, Ezzie,' and anyway Ezzie was already starting to walk faster down the sidewalk, holding his sandwich in the crook of his arm for safety.

'Race you, Benjie,' Ezzie said. It surprised Ezzie for a moment that he had said Benjie instead of Mouse. Then he broke into a run.

Garbage Dog was sitting in the shadow of the steps, but as soon as he heard the sound of running, he got up and came out quickly. He looked down the street. He saw the two boys running towards him, and after a minute Garbage Dog started running too.

Garbage Dog ran down the middle of the sidewalk. He heard the boys getting closer behind him and he ran faster. He was getting worried. The boys caught up with him, the three of them ran a few steps together, and then the boys passed. Ears back, Garbage Dog began to run faster. His wild eyes rolled to the two boys because he didn't know why they were running.

Then suddenly the boys slowed down to turn into the alley. Ezzie said, 'Here, G. D.,' and dropped the crust of his sandwich. Garbage Dog managed to stop. He came back and circled the crust.

'And here's something from me too.' Another piece of crust and a half slice of bologna.

Watching the boys, Garbage Dog began to eat. He saw the boys disappear laughing behind the bakery, and after a moment he hurried to join them.

About the Author

Betsy Byars was born in North Carolina, USA. Her father worked in a cotton mill, and Betsy went to school in a cotton-mill village. Her early aspirations were to work with animals, but then she married an engineering lecturer and moved to Illinois. While at home with her young children, Betsy began writing articles for newspapers and magazines. As the children started to read, so she began to write stories for them. Using her children's experience, and memories from her own childhood, she wrote over sixty books for young people.

Betsy Byars is a Newbery Medal winner and a National Book Award winner. Her books have appeared on the best books lists of the American Library Association, School Library Journal, and American Bookseller, among others. She now lives in South Carolina.